Shiva Naipaul was born in 1945 and educated in Trinidad and at University College, Oxford, where he read Classical Chinese. He based himself in London, but travelled widely in India, Africa, the Caribbean and the United States, where he spent a year as a Guggenheim Fellow. He died in London in 1985.

He was the author of *The Chip-Chip Gatherers* which won the Whitbread Award for Fiction, and *Fireflies*, winner of the Jock Campbell *New Statesman* Award, the John Llewellyn Rhys Memorial Prize and the Winifred Holtby Memorial Prize of the Royal Society of Literature in 1970. *A Hot Country*, his most recent novel, was published in 1983; he also wrote two books of non-fiction: *North of South* (1978) and *Black and White* (1980). *Beyond the Dragon's Mouth*, a collection of fictional and travel pieces, was published in 1984.

SHIVA NAIPAUL

An Unfinished Journey

SPHERE BOOKS LTD

Penguin Books Ltd, 27 Wrights Lane, London W8 5TZ (Publishing and Editorial)
and Harmondsworth, Middlesex, England (Distribution and Warehouse)
Viking Penguin Inc., 40 West 23rd Street, New York, New York 10010, USA
Penguin Books Australia Ltd, Ringwood, Victoria, Australia
Penguin Books Canada Ltd, 2801 John Street, Markham, Ontario, Canada L3R 1B4
Penguin Books (NZ) Ltd, 180–190 Wairau Road, Auckland 10, New Zealand

First published in Great Britain by Hamish Hamilton Ltd 1986
Published in Abacus by Sphere Books Ltd 1988

'Why Australia' first appeared in the *Sydney Morning Herald*; 'Flight into
Blackness' in *The Age*, Melbourne; 'My Brother and I' in *Gentleman's Quar-
terly*; 'The Illusion of the Third World' in the *Spectator*; 'The Death of
Indira Gandhi' in the *Observer*; and 'India and the Nehrus' in the *New
Republic*.

Made and printed in Great Britain by
Richard Clay Ltd, Bungay, Suffolk
Set in Ehrhardt

Contents

Introduction by Douglas Stuart   vii

Why Australia?   1

Flight into Blackness   11

My Brother and I   23

The Illusion of the Third World   31

The Death of Indira Gandhi   43

India and the Nehrus   53

An Unfinished Journey   65

Introduction

I first met Shiva Naipaul in the early spring of 1967. He was just twenty-two years old. My daughter introduced him – an Oxford friend, long-haired, slim and silent. By midsummer they were married and I was Shiva's father-in-law. Gradually we became friends, drawn together by a shared love of words, puns, jokes and ideas. His continuing intellectual growth astonished me. He loved books and his home was papered with them. What's more, he read them all, digesting the contents until their essence became part of him. But the paradox was that while his reading and comprehension were so rapid, his own writing was slow. He told me once that he would take a whole morning over a sentence and then reject it in the afternoon. Nevertheless he taught himself the discipline of journalism, meeting a deadline with the number of words required, without sacrificing his commitment to style and accuracy.

The final sentence in this book consists of the last words Shiva was to write. Before he could return to the typewriter, he was dead. The heart attack that killed him six months after his fortieth birthday also killed the book he had started and the novel he planned to write next. To dwell upon the waste would be otiose. There is already a body of his work in existence – three novels, two works of non-fiction and a collection of short stories and articles – to which can now be added the seven pieces, written in the last year of his life, that make up this book.

The six articles and the start of his book on Australia are not as haphazard as a first glance might suggest. They deal with Shiva's abiding preoccupations – his hatred of humbug, his search for identity, his consequent need to travel, his horror of every kind of racism and his fascination with India, the land of his ethnic origins. And it is typical of Shiva's oblique approach that he begins what was to be his book on Australia in Sri Lanka, preparing his reader for comparisons and paradoxes.

Before leaving on his Australian journey, we talked about the book he wanted to write. Shiva told me that he hoped to find an answer to the question; why didn't the Chinese, Japanese, Indians, Indonesians, Malayans and Filipinos find their way to the emptiness of Australia before the British? After all they were so much closer and yet so incurious about what might lie to the south. I don't know whether he followed the trail signposted by this question. Like other writers Shiva could say one thing and then watch his typewriter take him in a totally different direction. Certainly what seem to have caught his imagination in Australia were those whom he saw as being forced by white settlers into remaining 'stone age' aborigines. 'Flight into Blackness' challenges the whole concept of Australian *apartheid*.

On his return to London, Shiva had to leave almost at once for Trinidad and the funeral of a much-loved sister. Then – following the assassination of Indira Gandhi – he went to Delhi. Finally, settling down to write his book, Channel Four interrupted with a request for a television essay on a subject of his choice. 'The Illusion of the Third World' was the result. In all this bustle, I saw him infrequently. On one occasion, however, I did suggest to him that after the bleakness of his novel *A Hot Country* he might consider, in his book about Australia, returning to the comic vein he so skilfully exploited in *Fireflies* and *North of South*. His reply helps to pinpoint the watershed in Shiva's life as a writer. 'How can I?' he said. 'I have walked over the bodies in Jonestown.' Only his brother, he felt, fully understood what he was trying to do as a writer, and in this book Shiva explains what had been for him the basis of their complex relationship. It was not something over which he agonised. What he hoped to do was to clear up misconceptions. This removal of misconceptions was the central aim of all Shiva Naipaul's writing and these last seven pieces are not the least of his endeavour.

Douglas Stuart

Why Australia?

Sooner or later everyone I meet (or nearly everyone) will ask the question. Until it is asked we are at sea with one another. There exists an air of irresolution, of confusion; even, on occasion, of embarrassed tension. So, I wait for it to be posed. At last, at last it comes. There is the tell-tale knitting of the forehead, the inquisitorial tilt of the torso towards me. 'But *do* tell me why you chose (picked on/decided upon) Australia of all places?' I have had to endure variations on this theme for a decade. It has been put to me by Americans, Sri Lankans, Moroccans (who, not being satisfied with the answers I gave, deported me across the Strait of Gibraltar to Spain), Portuguese, Indonesians, Jamaicans . . . Itinerant writers tend to provoke a curiosity teetering on suspicion: a suspicion which can shade off into hostility. It is one of several occupational hazards I have learned to accept.

The cross-examination cannot be avoided. Day in, day out one has to cope with it. My response will be determined by my mood, by the circumstances and by my assessment of the merits of my challenger. Yet, it would be obtuse of me not to concede the naturalness of the inquiry. Consequently, it may be properly suggested that I am wrong to react so 'defensively' and to adopt stratagems of evasion. Why do I not come clean and explain my presence among you? There is an answer to that objection. It is this: when the question is posed I am being invited to categorise, to reduce to the abstractions of convenient, easily digested formulae an unprocessed and incomplete experience – an experience which I have not seriously attempted to categorise or to domesticate into the tidy units of expression commonly associated with the 'synopsis'. I have never mastered the art of composing synopses, a disability which has put me at a disadvantage in a society littered with the corpses of publicly funded artistic expression.

When I am asked the question, I am being invited, Immigration Officer style, to make public a declaration of my 'intentions', to state in accessible language what is often only dimly accessible to myself. In other words, the question, 'natural' though it is, is rooted in a misunderstanding of how a book comes into being and how a writer such as myself sets about his task. The question seeks to penetrate regions that ought to remain discreetly inviolable, whose obscurities ought to be respected. Still, I recognise that, no matter what I might say, the question will never go away. Why Australia? What kind of things/people are you interested in? What sort of book (a note of exasperation in the voice) are you *really* planning to write? Bearing in mind the things I have just said, I cannot guarantee satisfaction. But there is this consolation: Australia is not Morocco and so I have no immediate fears of deportation.

*

What, then, were my 'preconceptions?' What mental baggage did I bring with me when I stepped on to Australian soil for the first time? Perhaps the best approach to that enquiry is to provide an impressionistic account of my fluctuating perceptions of the continent. Back in the West Indies, as a boy growing up in Trinidad, Australia manifested its existence in a number of ways. Trivially, I recall the canned fruit served as a dessert after Sunday lunch. As I write this I see again the fruit-bowl on our dining-table, filled with pale pear slices soaked in a sugared syrup. More peculiarly, the ghee – clarified butter – my mother used in the preparation of certain dishes was also imported from Australia. That too came in tins. This Australian ghee perplexed me a little. I would wonder in a childish way why an ingredient so intimately associated with Indian cookery should come from so un-Indian a place. Was it possible that Australia, even in those distant days of utopian homogeneity, was already instinctively staking its now notorious claim to be considered 'part-of-Asia'?

A more direct form of contact was provided, of course, by cricket. We all knew about Don Bradman and accorded him our remote reverence. At some point in the fifties I remember an Australian team coming out to the West Indies. During the Test Match that was played in Trinidad my school operated on a 'half-day' system. Most of us made our way after lunch to the Queen's Park Oval and sat enthralled through a succession of burning afternoons. The Australians were particularly exotic birds of passage – exotic but, paradoxically, also imageless. Under their green caps they appeared to be even 'whiter' than the English touring teams with whom we were more familiar. Why this should have seemed so, I cannot say. Even more strangely (I suppose), echoes of that same impression of exaggerated 'whiteness' came back to me while travelling through Queensland. Maybe I was guilty of confounding the complexion of the people with the complexion of their politics. All the same, the blond pallor of many of those who are natives of the 'Sunshine State' is an arresting phenomenon, one that might repay investigation.

In early adolescence Australia infiltrated my consciousness in a more formal manner. Our geography lessons, imperial in scope and sentiment, did not neglect the Antipodes. At the age of twelve, sitting in some overwarm Port of Spain classroom, dressed in short khaki trousers and a blue shirt – at that time Trinidad's standard school uniform – I might have been discovered drawing maps of the wheat-rich Murray-Darling Basin. I knew about the Great Dividing Range, the Barrier Reef extending for hundreds of miles and the appalling desert heart of the 'Island-Continent', so impossibly far away from our little island located just a few miles off the Venezuelan coast; I knew that the rain-starved Island-Continent – from which came those pale sliced pears, those yolk-coloured halves of peaches that brought to a climax our Sunday lunches – had one of the lowest population densities in the world. . . . though I was never sure whether that assertion was a boast or a complaint.

We did not flatter ourselves in those days. It never entered our heads that the compliment might be returned; that Australian children, fellow denizens of an improbable Empire that blazoned itself in patches of red across maps of the world, might, in all fairness, be learning about our Northern Range (an expiring spur of the mighty Andean chain) and the sugar-cane plains watered by the Caroni River. We acknowledged, with unspoken candour, our humble status in the imperial dispensation. That self-effacement, I am now beginning to realise, may not have been entirely justified. 'Trinidad!' has come the exclamation from several people I have met along the way. 'Trinidad . . . now isn't that where the pitch-lake is?' It has been a surprising and gratifying discovery. The Empire has played strange tricks on us all. Bizarre familiarities surface in alien landscapes. (And I make no reference to the biggest trick – the bond of a common language.)

Incredulously, I learnt that sugar-cane was grown in Queensland. Sugar-cane! Cultivated and reaped by Europeans! In one of my text-books there was a photograph of a Queensland canefield. A man – European but not, I would guess, 'Anglo-Saxon' – stood nearby, holding what looked like a machete. He stared out from under the broad brim of his hat into the camera. I stared back at him unable to understand. How was that possible . . . socially possible . . . racially possible . . . ? Australia, scanty though its population, vast though its deserts, was a rich and blessed enclave. We were half-aware – I am not sure how we arrived at the knowledge – that it was a country set aside for the delectation of 'white men'; that, had we so wished, we could not have gone there. Why then were they growing sugar-cane? Sugar-cane, bitterest of crops, uprooter and enslaver of dark-skinned peoples, I associated with the human iniquities so prevalent in our tropical countryside. That anomalous photograph would worm its way into the deeper recesses of remembrance. There it would lie dormant – but not dead. A quarter of a century later I would be gazing out of the windows of a slow-moving train at the sugar-cane fields and sugar-cane towns of the Sunshine State. But I saw no labourers in broad-brimmed hats, no machetes, amid those acres gleaming with the silky arrows of a crop ready to be harvested.

Machines had subverted the bondage of mass muscular exertion. One man, operating levers in air-conditioned comfort, could scythe down acres in the course of a morning. In the sugar-cane towns of Northern Queensland I saw the modish bungalows of a prosperous bourgeoisie: two cars in the driveway, a tarpaulined boat beached in a garden, sprinklers watering trim lawns. Here were no lines of wooden barracks, no tumble-down shanties, no low-roofed mud huts thatched with grass. Here were no malodorous rum-shops, no women filling buckets at roadside stand-pipes, no tales of butchery and murder by cutlass. In the golden glitter of the morning, listening to the rustle of the wind through the canes, I felt I was hallucinating. These affluent cultivators had outlived the need to erect theories about the suitability of dark-skinned men for penitential labour in tropical zones; no longer was there any need to herd them into ships and transport them across the oceans. The descendants of the 'black-birded' Pacific Islanders had merely become a problem associated with the perils of 'multi-culturalism'. History plays cruel jokes on her children. Its outworn 'inevitabilities', its trumpeted 'necessities', rise up like mocking spectres. And another kind of darkness had prevailed in these suburban pastures.

'My father used to have Balts working here,' a farmer told me. 'Refugees from Europe, you know. *Balts* – that's what we called them in those days.' He looked out nostalgically across the fields he had inherited. He remembered one particular consignment of 'Balts' that had been sent to them. 'They couldn't speak a word of English. But they were all professional people, you know. In that group there was a doctor, a couple of lawyers, a musician, schoolteachers.' He smiled. 'They'd never seen a canefield before, never been in heat like this before, their hands were soft . . .' But sugar and sentiment have never been known to mix. They were put into barracks and issued with the simple tools of their new trade. For two years, those doctors and lawyers, musicians and schoolteachers had cut cane for his father. I thought of the photograph in my text-book, of the man staring out at me from the gloomy depths of his broad-brimmed hat. Who might he have been? I would have liked to listen to his story.

In the late sixties, I drifted down from Oxford to London and rented a one-roomed flat not far from the junk stalls and antique shops of the Portobello Road. I installed a little desk in a corner of the room overlooking the street. Shielded by dust-stiffened lace-curtains, I resumed work on the novel I had begun during my last term at Oxford. I wasn't to know it, but Australia was soon to re-enter my consciousness in a new and forceful way. The street, optimistically planted with spindly cherry trees, offered only two distractions. Directly opposite lived a lunatic of advanced middle-age. From time to time this demented individual would rattle open his sash window. Waving his arms, jumping up and down, he would scream his ritualistic curses into the summer sunshine. 'You yellow bastards. You goddamned yellow bastards!' Since coming to Australia, I have begun to see this man – a prisoner of the Japanese during the last war – in a new light. In London he was considered hopelessly mad. But, I am now forced to ask myself, wouldn't his incantations blend, without undue disturbance, into the obsessive demagoguery peddled by some of the more patriotic sects organised by ex-servicemen? Wouldn't his fear of the Yellow Peril (admittedly somewhat crudely expressed) be given a respectful hearing in the much-vaunted 'debate' about the threats posed by multi-culturalism? Lunacy, like beauty, exists only in the eye of the beholder.

The other distraction was more congenial. Now and again there appeared on the front steps of the house next door a good-looking woman. There, during bouts of warmer weather, she would sun herself. It was my wife who, over-hearing her speak, announced that our neighbours were

Australian. Her husband was an artist – an Australian-in-exile. For months, as if by mutual agreement, he and I did not speak. When our paths crossed – usually one of us would be going to or coming away from the local wine-shop – each would coyly look the other way. Eventually, through the good offices of a common friend, contact was made. At his dining-table, over the next few years, I was to meet a succession of Australians. The Island-Continent began to acquire a solidity, a kind of reality, it had not previously possessed. From their conversation I gleaned many curious facts. Sydney, I discovered, had its own Oxford Street and Paddington and Kings Cross. I regarded this as quaint and laughed. It is possible that I shouldn't have done so. As I listened to Australia-in-exile talk about itself, there emerged – perhaps it was not the intention – a portrait of a society given over to a reflexive philistinism that could border on barbarism.

I heard tales of anti-homosexual persecution; of young men with longish hair being set upon by gangs of thugs in public places; of the after-work stampede to the pubs. 'Ockerism' as I understood it, was a celebration of backwardness, a deliberate turning away from all forms of refinement and sophistication. The Ocker was allergic to human difference and variety; the derelict descendant of a denuded, amnesiac race that had hunted down Aboriginals for sport – you know . . . the boong, the blackfellow, the Murree, the wog, the coon . . . oh! . . . the infinite richness and vitality of our language – and, in verdant Tasmania, stooped to genocide. 'Up here,' confided a thonged, singletted youth I met in the Townsville mall, 'we are all racist.' He seemed proud of the fact. No good, said he whose breath smelled of beer, trying to help the Abos. 'We give them all this money and all they do is drink it away.' Rob that man of his racism and you rob him of everything. It would be an act of great cruelty to attempt to reform him. Take away his prejudice and you end up with the prototype of the crazed castaway – an Antipodean Ben Gunn, driven mad by the twin tyrannies of anonymity and nothingness. (In August of this year, Wilson

Mar, descendant of a long-settled Chinese family, flew in from Los Angeles to attend a reunion of his relatives. The event was reported in the *Australian*. 'He met,' the report said, 'the new Australian racism debate head on in a Cairns Street when a woman abused him for getting in her way and called him a "slope head"!' For whom should we feel the greater sadness – the abused or the abuser?)

It was during this period that I encountered Barry – Bazza – Mackenzie, the cartoon character created by Barry Humphries. For some years Mackenzie graced the pages of the English satirical fortnightly, *Private Eye*. I am aware that cultivated, self-conscious Australians have never been amused by this caricature of their fellow-countrymen. References to Bazza in politer circles brought forth frowns and murmurs of disapproval. Funny? Bazza Mackenzie *funny?* I needed my head examined. How disappointed they were to discover that such a deeply intelligent person as myself could find such unadulterated trash, such slanders, even mildly amusing. (How much nicer it is for the 'intellectual circles' of Sydney and Melbourne – again I am indebted to a report in the *Australian* – to be sent into an 'unprecedented frenzy' by the warblings of a French philosopher [yet another!] who had travelled all the way to Australia to tell them that they lived 'in an unreal world of images without meaning or value'.) To mention Bazza was – and still is – to court ostracism; to commit a social blunder of the first order: it was as if one had used the term 'nigger' in a room full of Africans.

I often used to wonder about these displays of aggravated sensitivity. Bazza's life – should I say 'lifestyle'? does that make it sound better? – could indeed be interpreted as having no meaning or value. But it doesn't follow that he either was or is 'unreal'. Whatever the case, I remain grateful to him. If nothing else, he enlarged my vocabulary. It was through his good offices I first came to know about 'galahs', 'sheilas', 'kookaburras', 'dunnies' (symbols – so I have read – of loneliness and isolation), 'norks' (his sister-in-law, Cherylene, was particularly well-endowed), 'ratbags', and other equally endearing and enduring features of the Australian scene. He drew back a veil which more delicate sensibilities had kept primly pinned down. The inept Bazza, foul-mouthed, beer-swilling, semi-literate and casually 'racist', stalked the streets of London seeking the fulfilment of his elementary desires, running into trouble, misunderstanding and defeats. It was not a pleasant portrait and the Australians I knew could not bear to look at him. They recoiled from him with cries of disdain and anguish. Untrue! Disgusting! But Bazza lives. I have met him again and again on my travels. He remains unready for nearly everything – including the promised land of the multi-cultural state.

*

I came the slow way to Australia.

In Sri Lanka, Singhalese and Tamils were slaughtering each other.

In the Philippines, civil order and decency had decayed and the discotheques of Manila transformed into temples of self-realisation.

In Malaysia, Chinese and Malays gazed without love at one another.

In Singapore, they fined you hundreds of dollars for the careless disposal of a matchstick, practised eugenics and read the works of Alvin Toffler, prophet of a future that required no past.

In overcrowded Java, they dreamt of transmigration, not of souls but of fecund bodies because the terraced amphitheatres of rice could no longer sustain the people. They wanted Lebensraum.

Everyone everywhere wanted to preserve their 'culture'; and, to do so, to preserve themselves from anonymity and nothingness, everyone everywhere seemed ready to resort or revert to barbarism.

My flight from Jakarta to Sydney stopped in Bali. Australians thronged into the aircraft. Two girls from Brisbane occupied the seats beside me. They produced, each her own, bottles of Southern Comfort and they giggled as they drank.

'Where're you from?' asked one of the girls.

I said I lived in London. Being weary, I did not elaborate. She said, 'I don't like Poms.'

As we flew into the gathering darkness, I was beginning – but only just – to understand the urges that had prompted so penitential a voyage of discovery.

Flight into Blackness

When, in 1872, Anthony Trollope visited Australia, the Aboriginal presence had shrunk to the margins of consciousness. For triumphant settlerdom, the derelict remnants of the dispossessed race no longer constituted a 'question' or a 'problem'. They did not even arouse curiosity or wonder. At best, they were the objects of morbid anthropological scrutiny. The Great Australian Silence had closed in about them. What the gun had started, indifference was bringing to completion. In scattered, isolated reserves out in the sticks, a handful of missionaries was doing what little could be done for the blackfellows, performing, it could be said, the obsequies for a race assumed by most to be doomed to extinction.

In 1872 imperial confidence, vigour and righteousness were in full flood. What would now be referred to as race relations seemed to have been arranged for all time. It was not a good time for those on the lower reaches of the evolutionary scale. Trollope wrote a big, tedious book about the Antipodean colonies. A modest chapter is devoted to the Aborigines. Their fate stirred in him neither compassion nor solicitude. ('The Aboriginal ... whom you are called on to kill, – lest he should kill you or your wife, or because he spears your cattle, – is to be to you the same as a tiger or a snake.') He mocked at those who, surrendering to vague sentiment, praised the dignified bearing displayed by many of the blackfellows. That alleged dignity of deportment, he retorted, represented nothing more than the trickery of a 'sapient monkey'. He was not moved by stories of faithfulness and devotion to duty: exceptional cases of constancy only served to highlight the innate worthlessness and shiftlessness of the race. The Aboriginal, the lowest of the low, was good for nothing; he was not even fit to be a servant, being 'infinitely lower' than the African Negro. The latter, in the cotton and sugar-cane fields of the New World, had demonstrated – under the firm governance of firm masters – his capacity for sustained manual labour. He had shown that he could be civilised into usefulness.

Trollope concedes, without a tremor of discomfort, that the land now so ripe with abundance was, in effect, the booty of dispossession; that Australia was no Terra Nullius, no empty quarter devoid of titles to ownership previous to the appearance of the Europeans. But then – so what? Could – should – what passes for natural justice be allowed to stand in the way of the expansion of the civilising instinct? Should Light, out of a nervous niceness about trespass, shrink before Darkness? The answer was obvious. The Aboriginal, condemned by his own degradation, impervious to improving influences, had sentenced himself. He had to go.

In Trollope's digressions on the Aborigines we see the civilising mission, the dogma of progress, in its most naked aspect. Theirs was to be a defeat without honour or remembrance, with no hint of possible redemption. His bland, brandy-and-water bonhomie adds to our unease. This prolix herald of Anglo-Saxon destiny is the most genial of exterminators – and not without a touch of philanthropy: the blacks, perish though they must, should, he avers, be allowed to slide into extinction 'without unnecessary suffering'.

If Trollope, a century ago, threatened to make the blacks the victims of his imperialist presumption, there are those in our own time who, moved by principles apparently in direct contradiction to those just outlined, are in no less danger of doing something similar. The contemporary mania for preservation, for the restoration of the timeless verities of culture and identity, is as disconcerting as Trollope's genocidal urges. In our day the Aboriginal has been costumed in the haute couture of prevailing intellectual fashion. He has been hailed as an ecological saint, obdurate freedom fighter, mystical dandy. Clothed in the garments of modish fantasy, he has emerged from the mists of forgetfulness.

Last year, towards the end of October, the discovery of a 'lost' Aboriginal clan was announced. Just how lost they actually were is debatable: one of the boys in the group was called Thomas. The excitement generated by this find would, one imagines, have appalled Trollope. The Central Land Council responded with militant rapture – it threatened to prosecute sightseers; anxiety was voiced about the clan's exposure to strange germs; it was rumoured that they were to be honoured by a visit from no less a personage than the Minister of Aboriginal Affairs. The anthropologists responded with caution (that boy Thomas!), sceptical about their scientific value. A reporter – the first on the scene – became almost lyrical in her attempt to describe these lost folk. They were, according to her, both statuesque and delicate of build, with skin of a translucent texture and eyes like deep pools. In a word, they were beautiful – ineffably so. Their nakedness contrasted favourably with the clothes worn by their domesticated brethren living in the out-station to which they had come. These newcomers of lustrous eye and skin had yet to be 'taught shame by the white man'.

Another writer, however, seemed a little piqued with the lost tribe. Their 'coming in' defied the trend towards going out. Across Australia, the Aborigines were on the move, turning their backs on the missions and stations, heading away from contact with a civilisation that had never done them any good. Only when he was allowed to do 'a bit of hunting and food-gathering' did the black begin to recover his spiritual wholeness and reality. The black, it would appear, became himself only when he was restored to some semblance of his original condition and was again a primitive. I use this last term with caution – it had got me into a lot of trouble – though I am not sure why it should be objectionable to so describe those elemental activities associated with nomadism in the desert places.

The writer's ideal Aboriginal (very sad, very lost) talks in a dilapidated patois. ' . . . Want to go back west, me been thinking. I been worry and worry for my country . . .' It is odd that the quest for authenticity – at any rate in this case – should be coupled to the threadbare rags of a pidgin English which robs the individual of the power of self-expression; a self-expression no doubt available to him in his own language, whose locutions – presumably – could be rendered into grammatical English. But, I suppose, if this were done, his gain in lucidity would be balanced by a diminution of effect. The quasi-romantic belief in an ahistorical Aboriginal essence, beyond the reach of time, beyond – even – the reach of language, is well displayed in the writer's testy sentimentality.

The Great Australian Silence has been replaced by the Great Australian Confusion.

*

In Darwin, when I was there last September, they were doing their best to celebrate National Aborigines Week. On a pearly morning of drizzle, I stirred myself and went to Raintree Square in the malled heart of the town to have a look at one of the advertised events marking the festivities. A modest crowd had gathered – mostly tourists, I guessed, in search of casual diversion: in the Northern Territory, as in Queensland, the Aboriginal cause seems to lack popular appeal. The bony, skin-blemished woman given to playing Waltzing Matilda on her violin had not strayed from her chair in the mall. Her scrapings threaded a thin vein of lacklustre patriotism through the humid morning.

I myself, let it be admitted, was not in a suitably celebratory frame of mind. A day or two before, the Northern Land Council, acting on advice tendered them by a couple of anthropologists (at least so they called themselves) of expatriate extraction and a woman of mixed descent (who had taken exception to my remarking over dinner in a Chinese restaurant that the Aborigines could not be considered to have created a culture as sophisticated – say – as the Chinese or Greeks or Indians or Egyptians had done) . . . the

Northern Land Council had banned me from the territories under its control. They had heard, one of their spokesmen later clarified, that I had said the Aborigines were a primitive race. 'The people' had been much incensed to learn this – a process of consultation that could only have been telepathic – and had taken appropriate action against me. Under no circumstances, he added, would 'the people' reverse their decision.

'So,' I had said to the woman of mixed descent, 'you run a police state.'

'Yes,' she replied. 'And we're proud of it.'

So, alas, my view of the Aboriginal cause had been sharpened.

The contest for restitution which, at first, had seemed so pleasantly quixotic a crusade assumed after that episode the depressingly familiar lineaments of so-called liberation struggle the world over; had become, I began to understand, an excuse for excess and empty posturing. To pretend to believe that the Aboriginal (I employ the term in its loosest, everyday meaning) is, or can be, anything other than a petitioner at the impregnable gates of 'White Australia', to endow with undue credibility such rhetorical manifestations of autonomy as a separate flag, colourful 'tent embassies', calls for treaties and the like, is to encourage the drift to delusion and eventual political disaster. Insignificant though it might be in itself, my banishment by fiat in the name of 'the people' was a symptom of decay. Still, the Northern Land Council deserved to be congratulated: theirs – and I have travelled fairly extensively over the face of the planet – was the first such banning order that had ever been imposed on me. I expect I ought to have been more amused than I was at the time.

Standing in the drizzle, an uncharitable sourness of expression marring my usual affability, I watched the confused preparations for the morning's entertainment. Varied excitements would be enlivening the coming week. The first ever National Aboriginal Art Award was to be handed out; there were to be exhibitions of traditional dancing and singing and music; less traditionally, there would be film and video shows, a street march, a football match; a baby show was planned as was a family day replete with 'bush foods'. Elderly, (genuinely) Aboriginal men and women were sprawled under the trees, their dusty legs stretched out like blackened sticks before them. They contemplated the city scene with a bemused, abandoned gaiety. Among them, foreheads banded with the red, black and yellow insignia of the cause, moved a number of energetic white females, ministering to the comforts of their clientèle, exuding an air of ferocious amiability as they chatted and laughed with and caressed the tangled heads of their charges.

Television cameras swayed above the heads of the moistened crowd. At one end of the little square, a banner proclaimed that the Earth was the (Aboriginal) Mother. ('Our lifestyle,' said a native member of the Territory's Legislative Assembly, 'reflects the environment through our dreamings and our emotional and physical well-being are determined by the need to be in harmony with our natural environment.') I spotted one of my adversaries, the white Press Officer of the Northern Land Council.

He was a strange young man. Simultaneously, he managed somehow to be both dour and emotional. For him – and I speak without rancour – the cause had inflated itself into a cultic attachment. On one occasion he had grown misty with feeling while telling me how Aboriginal children of mixed parentage had, within living memory, been forcibly taken away from their homes, herded on to trucks, hosed down; and, thus sanitised, sent off to institutions to be re-educated in the ways of the white man. It was not his ardour of which I disapproved but, rather, the assumption that such wrongs eliminated the need for all further introspection. His retrospective 'white' pain, his guilt, sufficed, nullifying any enquiry that might threaten to sour his commitment. Like all cultists, his behaviour was erratic, veering about as devotional duty dictated. You could never tell what he was thinking because, by his own admission, he didn't think a great deal. A slave to his emotions, he merely served.

Under a tree some blacks were setting up an array of technical equipment – drums, electrical guitars, amplifiers. There was a surge of interest when a man, naked to the waist, loins wrapped in a cloth, skin powdered, arrived with a didgeridoo. The cameramen and sound recordists converged upon him. With some difficulty (the inventors of the didgeridoo couldn't have been expected to anticipate this particular challenge), he managed to aim his unwieldy instrument at a microphone and embark on a sequence of hollow trumpetings. When he was done, there was enthusiastic applause, mainly from the urban section of the gathering. Perhaps encouraged by this, he started up again. A pretty girl of mixed descent, her torso wrapped in the folds of an Aboriginal flag, paraded around the fringes of the square. To more applause the didgeridoo player, having completed his encore, retired from the scene. His place was taken by a troupe of daubed dancers. Again the cameramen and sound recordists converged. My attention was seduced by another adolescent of indeterminate race whose T-shirt was emblazoned with the epicene features of Michael Jackson. I watched her watching the daubed dancers, stomping out, I presumed, rhythms rooted in the Dreamtime. Her expression was no different from that worn by most of the assembled tourists – a sort of puzzled, faintly respectful, faintly embarrassed diffidence. Was the Earth really her Mother? Was her emotional and physical well-being really determined by her need to be in harmony with the natural environment?

The oratory began. After several months in Australia I was familiar enough with its content (. . . forty thousand years of culture . . . the death symbolised by landlessness . . .) to be able to pay only intermittent attention. It was impossible not to take account of the fact that most of the speakers were of mixed ancestry and of comparatively light complexion; individuals whose aboriginality had undergone progressive dilution over generations. None of them looked as if they had done a bit of hunting and food-gathering. Not recently anyway. How real could the connection be between these citified gentry of the cause and those dusty, stick-legged, dark-skinned ones who squatted so patiently on the flag-stones? By what bonds of sympathy and desire and cultural affinity were they linked?

'This is the decade of the Aboriginal,' shouted one of the speakers.

'Right on! Right on!' chorused the girl in the Michael Jackson T-shirt.

'The land doesn't belong to us,' shouted a woman of Chinese cast of countenance. 'We belong to the Land.'

'Right on! Right on!'

The flag-draped girl, unfurling herself, skipped around the square.

The members of the band twanged their guitar strings, peered at the dials on their consoles, adjusted levels. Later that morning in Raintree Square, forty thousand years of culture, of sacred communion with the Antipodean earth, blossomed into the amplified rhythms of Country and Western music.

I drifted slowly back through the steamy morning to my hotel, going past the pub consecrated not to forty thousand years of Aboriginal culture but to two centuries of Aboriginal defeat: there, behind the glass doors, over glasses of beer and rough wine, the last rites were being played out.

*

It is one thing to reinterpret and rewrite the Aboriginal past, to reach a new understanding of the virtues (and vices) of a society so long ignored and denigrated: Trollopian presumption deserves to be discredited. No harm is done if the settler kingdom should experience tremors of anxiety and see its own past in a different, less than heroic light. Self-knowledge may be alarming, but without it we remain in a state of arrested development, prey to spurious vanities not worth the cost of the ink and the stone used to celebrate them. But it is quite another thing, in the name of restitution, to deform our vision of the present and its needs, to invoke afresh cultures and identities ravaged by time and contact and powerlessness. These attempted acts of restoration are not merely dishonest: they are cruel. Too much has happened.

I am prepared to believe that there are many Aborigines who wish to escape the clutches of the settler state, to take themselves out into the desert places – if only at weekends – and do their thing. The sublimated racism that underwrites and encourages this phenomenon is highly amusing, if only because its theorists would recoil in horror from the suggestion that they were guilty of any such dereliction. But how else is one to interpret this confining of the Aboriginal in his aboriginality? There are, of course, a dozen fashionable ways of dressing up this flight from the burdens of reality. Ours is an age cursed with the impulse to self-realisation and our vocabulary is rich. (In Australia, as I discovered, self-realisation extends even to the vegetation of the place: there are those who would expel every alien growth and plant gum trees and salt bush everywhere: the landscape too must be allowed to be true to itself.) But the escape into an adventure playground of timelessness, of goannas and kangaroos and red earth, the running off into a world of unalterable Aboriginal essences – this racially based tuning in and dropping out – is a condescending and profoundly flawed prescription for regeneration. Either the Aboriginal is or is not a citizen of Australia. And if he is (which is the case) he must face the consequences. It is not a 'race' that cries out for rescue, but the victims of a historical process, thousands of men and women and children.

When even lost tribes who have not yet been taught shame by the white man harbour in their midst little boys called Thomas, we ought to take pause. The modern world is too near, too pressing. At best, atavism is a harmless fantasy, not sustainable with any degree of persistent realism under skies criss-crossed by satellites and jet aircraft; at its worst, it must be considered a tragedy – a failure of nerve. Defeat ought not to be confounded with, or explained away by, self-realisation. In any case, the call of the wild certainly cannot provide any answers for those – the majority – with substantial infusions of Chinese or Irish or Scottish blood. It takes a practised eye to discern the aboriginality of many of these town-dwelling, Christianised, Australianised representatives of the 'race' whose genetic exoticism and de facto 'assimilation' make absurd all those claims to mystical sensibilities and vulnerabilities.

When I was in the pastoral town of Rockhampton, I heard a most singular *cri de coeur* from an improbable quarter. The Cattlemen's Association wanted to find out who decides who is an Aboriginal. Could someone, preferably someone in Canberra – one of the chief sacred sites of the cause – *please* tell them. My heart was not wrung by their perplexity. The cattlemen of Rockhampton were, I think, being a trifle hypocritical and ingenuous. The settlerdom of which, historically, they were so conspicuous a vanguard, whose pioneering exploits had swollen into tales of mythological proportions, had sown the seeds of their trumped-up dilemma by contemptuously assigning to the wilderness of aboriginality anyone with the slightest admixture of indigenous blood. Their forebears were among those who had carried out the original classification.

The cause of the cattlemen's distress was plain enough. Apart from the restitutional terrors of Land Rights and Sacred Sites (provoking nightmares of sudden dispossession), they looked with tax-paying despair at the amount of money being expended on Aboriginal uplift and comfort. Nowadays in Australia it pays to be 'Aboriginal'. Hearts ache for those millions of dollars lavished on such bodies as the National Aboriginal Conference, the Aboriginal Development Commission, the Institute of Aboriginal Studies and so on. The cattlemen shake their heads at all those programmes for Aboriginal Health, Aboriginal Employment, Aboriginal Legal Aid, Training, Culture, Recreation, 'Social Support'. Indignant voices clamour. Who are these so-called Aboriginals? *Please* tell us!

Yet, whatever the motives of those who ask it, the question is a good one. After two hundred years of European occupation and culture shock, it is a question that even a 'full blood' (defined thus by my Australian dictionary: '1. an individual of unmixed ancestry esp. for dark-skinned peoples as Aborigines, negroes etc. 2. purebred, esp. of horses') might well put to himself. But he can only do so with profit if he is allowed – and allows himself – to break free from the sublimated racism that would imprison people in their imagined essences; that would convert into a kind of substance that mockery of an idea summed up by the term 'black'. (We can say the same about the use of 'white'. The man who is merely 'white' is no less a prisoner than the man who is merely 'black'.) Racial metaphysics is a cul-de-sac.

What should I, in the light (perhaps I should say darkness) of this debased coding, make of myself? I am, after all, a man of 'full-blooded' Indian ancestry. Should I therefore put on a dhoti? Should I take myself up to a cave in the foothills of the Himalayas and surrender myself to the contemplation of the transmigration of souls? After a century of separation from the motherland, a century of confusion and disintegration, my racial essence has offered no clues to the dilemmas I have had to face. In Sydney I met a young man of Mediterranean complexion and feature. In fact, he was partly of Spanish ancestry – but, of course, he referred to himself as 'Aboriginal'. He was well-educated, urbane, at ease in every way – so far as I could tell – with the life of the city. This young man wanted to be an artist. He showed me some of his work. I stared, with intensifying incredulity and sadness, at his drawings of serpents, enigmatic birds, lizards . . . resurrected out of the Dreamtime. Such was his art; such was his universe of 'meaningfulness'. It was in Sydney too that I saw a little group of Aboriginal Rastafarians standing on a street corner. Not for them the Dreamtime, but mere universalised blackness. 'I and I want to be free,' declaimed an Aboriginal poetess, resorting to the Rastafarian dialect of her Jamaican brothers, ' . . . for I Aborigine . . . Never will I lose my identity . . .' So she chanted at the official opening of an Aboriginal Arts Centre in one of Sydney's inner districts.

The flight into aboriginality, into blackness, is a flight into despair; an escape from the challenges of history.

My Brother and I

Men have played a comparatively small part in my life. My father died when I was seven and I was brought up by and among women: my mother and my sisters. At an early age I came to know what there was to know about crinolines, the shapes of skirts and blouses, and the various do-it-yourself techniques of styling hair: my sisters sewed their own clothes and never – or hardly ever – patronised hairdressers. The effect this matriarchal environment has had on my character is not easy to assess. Certainly, I never much cared for Westerns and developed a dislike for rough games; I enjoy (though by no means exclusively so) the company of women and am responsive to the tidal motions of their moods – their curious gaieties and darknesses and deceptions; and, without consciously intending it, I see that they have had a major role in my fiction.

What one might call the male principle was almost entirely absent during my childhood. True, I was taught mainly by men, but they were merely distant figures of authority. They never entered intimately into my emotional and imaginative life. I must suppose, given the nature of the household in which I was reared, they were beyond my grasp as male creatures. And yet – paradoxically – the expectations and terrors that dominated my childhood and adolescence were shaped by the legends left behind by a shadowy man: a man whose voice I never heard, whose face I could never adequately picture to myself. For, in a mysterious city referred to as London, there lived a brother. A brother! Sometimes I would fall to wondering about that remote and mysterious entity. A brother ... *my* brother ... That such a person actually existed, that such a person could exist, bordered on the incredible. I could not grasp the reality represented by the term 'brother'. It eluded all my meditations, ran away like quicksilver from all the traps I laid for it. I would end by playing with the syllables of the word, letting them dance about on my tongue, until they were reduced to a rill of babbling, meaningless sound. (I used to play the same game with the word 'saucer': the resulting chaos was both amusing and alarming.)

This brother, who was so notional a being, was known to me mainly by his relics: a framed water-colour in our sitting-room; ageing text-books with his signature scrawled across the blankness of yellowing title-pages; a photograph in my mother's bedroom. Beyond these there was a memory picture. The details are hazy and I cannot vouch for their accuracy. It was the day of his departure for England. We had travelled out from Port of Spain to Trinidad's little bungalow of an airport – then a most exotic place: in those days virtually everyone who went abroad travelled by ship. We must have discovered that the aircraft was going to be late, for I recall us leaving the airport and driving to the house of a relative who lived not too far away. The picture fades at this point. When next it comes to life, I am sitting in a car parked on a narrow road running along close to the airstrip. Childish memory recreates one of those Trinidad afternoons of burning heat, glare, heat-waves making watery mirages on the asphalt; I seem to remember how the wind stirred the wild grasses growing along the verges. An aircraft was standing on the runway. 'Look! Look!' Someone – presumably my brother – was waving a handkerchief at us from a port-hole. I seem to recall too the roar of the engines, the aircraft climbing into a blank, blue sky, becoming smaller as it rose higher, shrinking into an ever-diminishing point of metallic glitter . . . disappearing.

I would have been about five years old at the time – the baby of the family. On that day my brother had disappeared into regions unknown to me; and so became, as I have said, cloaked with an unreality I found impenetrable. But this unreality, however abstract, however bloodless, was loaded with implication for me. My brother, by reason of his academic successes, had established a pattern, a set of standards. Willy-nilly, these were transformed into a sort of Absolute – small-island, colonial style: willy-nilly, my character, my actual performance, my 'promise', would be judged against the expectations generated by that Absolute. *He* had won an 'Exhibition' (a type of scholarship) to a good secondary school. Would *I? He* had won a Trinidad Government scholarship that had taken him to Oxford. Would *I?* Invariably – how could it be otherwise? – I suffered by comparison. No one ever quite lives up to the demands of an Absolute. You gaze into mirrors – school reports, other faces, overheard opinions – and all you ever see reflected are your own inadequacies; the treasons you are alleged to have inflicted on a self-contained, self-sustaining regime of preconceived and unexamined expectations. I became 'sensitised' at an early age to discourtesy and stupidity. Those without imagination are doomed to these twin vices. Looking back on myself, I see that I was a difficult, moody and enigmatic child. It was a form of self-protection against the tyrannies that sought to imprison me, that offered me neither compassion nor courtesy. And – perhaps – the child has developed into a difficult, moody and enigmatic man. He doesn't like to think he is . . . but he recognises, glancing into the mirrors that offer themselves, he may be.

Incidents come to mind – some of which still cause me pain. There was that most august relative of mine who (I was probably about ten years old at the time), when I baulked at eating with my hands – I can no longer remember what led up to that petty action of rebellion – remarked: 'Wait until *you* get to Oxford. *You* haven't got in there yet. Remember that.' Now, even at so tender an age, could I possibly forget? Even more painful was an outburst by the headmaster at my secondary school. I was behaving skittishly and, quite correctly, he became angry. 'You must think,' he screamed at me, with a bizarre, rising rage, 'that you too have already written some books. Well, let me tell you – you haven't!' I was shocked by his rancour, by his malice. More shocked than I would have been if he had hit me. But it doesn't do to dwell on such delinquencies.

Of course, the flesh-and-blood brother, the young man whom I had seen waving a handkerchief from the port-hole of an aircraft, disappearing into the sky in a final flash of sun on metal, had no direct connection with any of these oppressions. I was dealing with a doppelgänger – but, alas, during those years, the doppelgänger was all I knew. Or pretty nearly all I knew. Sometimes, the postman arrived with blue air-mail letters, the cause of much excitement in our household. Once, a couple of books arrived for me – an illustrated history of science and (I believe) a book about the young Walter Scott. Occasionally, I would listen with a kind of dazed astonishment to this notional being – *my* brother! – reading a short story on the radio: in those days the BBC still had a Caribbean Service. But none of these stray items allowed me to construct a picture. In fact, they only aggravated my confusion. When I was about eleven, this mysterious figure suddenly arrived among us. Why he should thus manifest himself, I had no idea. Still, it was an interlude of wonder; of intense excitement for me. I would go and stand in the doorway of his bedroom and gaze curiously upon him as he lay on the bed, smoking cigarettes out of a green tin. The tableau revived my father's fading image. He too, in the warm, quiet afternoons, would lie on that same bed, reading and smoking cigarettes. We must have talked, but I can no longer remember what we talked about. One day I showed him a childish story I had written out in a copy-book. It was about a boy – an English boy – running away to sea. This narrative I had begun in the third person and, quite unconsciously, ended in the first. (I had stumbled on to one of the tricks of 'modernism' without effort.) He pointed this out to me, at the same time praising the endeavour. Then he went away again.

Abstraction only began to lessen when I myself went to England (even unto Oxford!) at the age of eighteen. Yet, the gap of twelve or thirteen years that separates us remained important. We did not, overnight, cease to be strangers to one another. He perplexed me; and I, no doubt, perplexed him. We had, after all, come out of different worlds. The Hindu Trinidad of his youth was not the Hindu Trinidad of my youth. We did not have a shared past; we did not have a shared pool of memory, ancestral or otherwise. I had vulnerabilities he did not always find easy to understand. Our natural ties of affection would have to discover new modes of expression – and, for a long time, neither of us knew what those might be; for a long time there was mutual distress. No grand solutions have ever occurred. But there have been a series of small resolutions along that difficult, treacherous road. We have come to recognise each other's autonomy, to acknowledge the existence of areas of privacy and inaccessibility. Writing has helped, not hindered, that process of slow accommodation. It has offered a means of communication.

Given what I have said about the tyrannies of comparison, my choice of career must seem like an exercise in masochism. Why didn't I become a fireman? an engineer? a traffic warden? I cannot deny that it has provided a fertile field for mindless malice. There have been those who have hinted that I am doing no more than 'imitate' my brother. I can think of at least one English critic who, in his comments on my most recently published novel, showed himself not above this slander. He did not understand the book – and therefore, being human, resorted to calumny. Our sentimental, left-wing friends are not always compassionate. They know how to stick the knife in. (Their rewards are lavished on those who tell them that the British government is preparing concentration camps for its immigrant minorities; that Nazism squats on our doorsteps.) I think I prefer the genial Trinidadian who once put forward the hypothesis that my brother actually wrote my books for me.

Truth to tell, I never made a decision to become a 'writer'. It happened. Or, rather, it began to happen slowly and haltingly, fed by despair. The event, such as it was, occurred during my last year at Oxford when it was clear that the academic pretensions which I had brought with me to the University were dead beyond dreams of resurrection; when it was starkly apparent that soon I would be venturing out into a world where I would be equipped to do nothing. During that last year I had become ill with apprehension. Until then I had made little or no pretence about being a 'writer'. I had had no contact with Oxford's ambitious literary and theatrical circles; been involved with no student magazine or newspaper. I had served no recognisable apprenticeship; I had nothing in common with the young men and women heading down to London, optimistic and bright-eyed from the champagne farewells enacted on a dozen College quadrangles. That final year, I lived in foggy apprehension. And what turned out to be a 'career' started, so to speak, of itself. It began as I was sitting at my desk, staring at a page of Chinese characters (I was doing a degree in Chinese), which danced meaninglessly across the frail paper . . . it began when, for no reason I can fathom, a sentence came into my head. 'The Lutchmans lived in a part of the city where the houses, tall and narrow . . .'

I pushed away the books and papers in front of me, wrote down the sentence and started to follow it. At that moment I was propelled by inquisitiveness, not by literary anticipation. I wanted to see where – how far– that sentence would take me. It took me a long way. To suggest that I left Oxford with a vocation would be an exaggeration. What I did take with me was a possibility of further adventure with that sentence which had presented itself to me so gratuitously. Another two years would pass before it unwound itself to a climax, before I could say I had written a 'book'. There was something modestly miraculous about that *ligne donnée*. It gave me a reason to go on existing.

The paradox is this: I was doing anything but following in my brother's footsteps when I started to write. Rather, I had taken the first step on the road to independence, to the autonomy that had always been denied me. I was breaking loose of the doppelgänger absolutism which had so marred and scarred my childhood. If the decision to write had been a consciously formulated one – then I could be legitimately accused of courting masochistic experiences. That, however, was not the case. I do not write out of a desire to 'imitate' anyone, nor out of any desire to maintain a family 'tradition'. If I write, it is because I have to; because there is nothing else I can do; because it is the only way I have of trying to understand the world in which I live. In other words, I write out of necessity. I do not regard literature as a genteel pastime. Nor do I regard it as a lucrative 'dialogue' between oppressed and former oppressor.

None of this, let it be understood, is intended as a denial of my brother. I am not attempting either to deny or to downplay my admiration for his work. He has served as an example and as an exemplar. But we are each our own man. I acknowledge that comparisons between us are bound to occur. It would be very strange if two men, both of denuded Indian ancestry, both born on the same island, both with roughly similar concerns, both exercising the complementary arts of fiction and journalism . . . it would be very strange if comparisons were not drawn: my only objection is to doppelgänger absolutism. Our being brothers is interesting. But it is not intrinsically so. In the end, it is the work that matters, not the relationship.

The Illusion of the Third World

We do not see people as they are any more. Instead, we see
– or learn to believe that we see – those ghostly entities we call
'relationships'. There's me, there's you – and, somewhere in
the middle, there's our relationship. And of all the relationships that there are, none is more problematic or contentious
than that between the rich and the poor, the developed and
the underdeveloped, the advanced and the backward, the
'North' and the 'South'. Or, to employ one of the most
entrenched buzz-words of our time, there is no relationship
more problematic or contentious than that posed by those
hundreds of millions of human beings lumped together by
the term 'Third World'.

I have always had trouble with the concept. To be candid,
I consider it distasteful. In search of guidance, I turned to
my menagerie of up-to-date dictionaries. The notion being
of comparatively recent coinage, there was no point in looking
in any of the more traditional compilations. According to my
American dictionary, the Third World is 'a group of nations,
especially in Africa and Asia, that are not aligned with either
the Communist or the non-Communist blocs'. It further adds
that the Third World can be construed as 'the aggregate of
the underdeveloped nations of the world'. My *British*
dictionary, extending the geographical sweep, defines the
Third World as comprising 'the countries of Africa, Asia and
Latin America especially when viewed as underdeveloped
and as neutral in the East-West alignment'. My *Australian*
dictionary was even more expansive – to the point of being
chatty. For it, the Third World signifies the 'developing
countries especially in Africa, South America and South-
East Asia, which are not heavily industrialised, have a low

standard of living and are usually not politically aligned with either the Communist or the non-Communist blocs'.

One, I suppose, gets the general drift of the idea intended to be conveyed. Yet, even in these elementary sketches, there are obvious discrepancies. Why the Americans should omit Latin America from their list and the Australians should point the finger at South-East Asia is, to me at any rate, slightly puzzling. The South and Central American states are not, by all accounts, heavens on earth. Nicaragua is trying hard to be non-aligned but is experiencing some difficulty. Singapore, on the other hand, is a model of East Asian assiduity. I was there not long ago and marvelled at the tall buildings, the troughs of flowers adorning the highway from the airport, the cleanliness of the streets, the traffic regulations. No one in their right mind would accuse Singapore of being a Third World country. You'd probably be deported if you had the boldness to imply anything of the kind. Alas, there is no doubt about Africa. From the desert shores of the Mediterranean to the jungly banks of the Limpopo, from Somalia to Sierra Leone, the continent is a show-case of despair. Indeed, if it weren't for Africa, it's just conceivable that the whole concept of a Third World reality might collapse into disrepute.

And what about that other apparently essential attribute of Third Worldhood – non-alignment? It presents us with one of those dilemmas which, one imagines, would delight an Oxford linguistic philosopher. We could put the question this way: how many different varieties of alignment can you accommodate within the idea of non-alignment without robbing it of meaning altogether? The answer hasn't yet been found, and – perhaps – never will be. Non-alignment, in practice if not in theory, displays some truly remarkable properties. It is as puzzling as the nature of light which – so quantum mechanics tells us – sometimes behaves as though it were composed of discrete particles, and sometimes as though it were composed of waves. A similar bewilderment descends when we contemplate the non-aligned. Some are non-aligned towards Moscow, some are non-aligned towards

Washington; some, fluctuating between wave and particle, smile at Washington, frown at Moscow, and gratefully accept pandas from Peking; some are unashamedly capitalist, some are quasi-Marxist; some offer hospitality to Communist soldiery, some have American 'advisers' – the Americans, since Vietnam, confining themselves to advice; some are socialist democracies, some are free-enterprise dictatorships; some interfere in the internal affairs of others and some don't; some only surface at conference time. The possibilities are infinite. What I've just said only scratches the surface.

A quick sampling from the conference of the non-aligned held in Delhi in 1983 will help to illustrate the point. Venezuela, because of its border dispute with neighbouring, non-aligned Guyana, held aloof. Burma too seemed to be displeased – though I am not sure why. Still, despite these defections, ninety-nine countries were represented. Afghanistan was present, as was that other vocal champion of non-alignment, Cuba. A Cambodian delegation showed up, though whether it represented the non-aligned Vietnamese-backed faction or the non-aligned freedom-fighting faction I cannot say. Iran came – and Iraq came. Ethiopia, which used to be non-aligned with Washington but is now non-aligned with Moscow, turned up; Somalia, which used to be non-aligned with Moscow but is now non-aligned with Washington, did not turn up – but I can see no reason why it shouldn't have done. Lebanon, whose internal alignments baffle us all, managed to put together a delegation. Sri Lanka, ignoring the civil war between its Tamil minority and its Singhalese majority, demonstrated its solidarity: whether it would do so now that its relations have cooled with non-aligned India – which it accuses of collaboration with the non-aligned Tamil separatists – is a matter of conjecture. Statehood, as was made evident at the conference, is not a necessary prerequisite. Both the Palestine Liberation Organisation and the South-West Africa People's Organisation attended. Nor is it necessary to be an acknowledged Third World country, as is demonstrated by the perennial prominence of Yugoslavia and the ambiguous pretensions of the flirtatious Swedes. Neither of the Chinas was there – Taiwan because its existence isn't recognised by most of the non-aligned states, and the People's Republic because it is an alignment in itself.

Still, whatever the confusions, we do, I believe, have a picture of the exemplary Third World denizen: he lives a hand-to-mouth existence, he is indifferent to the power struggles of the mighty ones and he is dark-skinned. I will, however, return later to the vexed question of his colour. That such people do exist – and that there are unnumbered millions of them – no one can deny. We live in a fantastical world; a world in which the divergences between different groups of men have become so great, have been so magnified, that there seems no possibility of bridging the abyss between those who can land men on the moon and those who would be hard put to it to invent a tin-opener. African famine, dramatic and horrifying, is today the pre-eminent symbol of Third Worldhood. Those slow-moving files of refugees in stony landscapes, those motionless babies with flies clustered round the eyes – images like these belong to the realm of nightmare. They simultaneously arouse our compassion and debase our conception of the victim, who is seen as passive, dependent – the skeletal receptacle of what our charity can provide. I do not decry charity. If a man is drowning we must rescue him. But charity has its dangers. Chief among them is condescension. We have been kind, we congratulate ourselves, to the 'starving millions'. But who are they, these emblematic multitudes? Is it not possible that the abstractions in which we deal end, despite all our kindnesses, in further diminishing those whom we sincerely wish to help?

The Third World is a form of bloodless universality that robs individuals and societies of their particularity. In the spirit of charity we go forth and denude them. Adapting the opening sentence of Leo Tolstoy's *Anna Karenina*, we might say that each society, like each family, is unhappy in its own way. Even Ethiopia, despite the almost abstract extremity of its condition, has its own unique tale to tell – a story of feudal monarchy, coup d'état, civil war. To blandly subsume, say, Ethiopia, India and Brazil under the one banner of Third Worldhood is as absurd and as denigrating as the old assertion that all Chinese look alike. People only look alike when you can't be bothered to look at them too closely.

The promiscuous idea of a Third World does not stand up to close examination. Rather like Count Dracula confronted by the Cross, it crumbles away. Lacking particularity, it delineates nothing that really exists. It is a flabby Western concept lacking the flesh and blood of the actual. And that flesh-and-blood actuality, rising up out of dark recesses, frequently overrides and mocks what is apparently reasonable. We impute to the 'starving millions' the elementary physical desires suggested by their elementary physical needs. But it is also important to understand the dreams of men, for their dreams may transcend the provision of unpolluted water supplies, decent roads and hospitals. More regularly than we would like, other obscurer needs and impulsions surface into the outer air as bats do from their roosts at twilight. Yet again, Moscow and Washington are forced to look on impotently as the Third World created by their imaginations puts on the exotic robes suited to multifarious and unsuspected fantasies of redemption and self-expression; yet again they watch as carefully wrought foreign policies melt away into oblivion, as favoured leaders fly off into exile or are killed in their palaces.

Men do not live by bread alone. In the Central African Republic, Jean Bokassa transforms his state into an Empire and declares himself its Emperor. He orders a golden crown; a bejewelled throne; he adorns himself in velvets. The French laugh, but they supply the goods. In the First World business is business. Nevertheless, are we entirely certain that Bokassa's subjects shared our sense of absurdity? They may not have. Not all that far away from the Central African Empire – in Uganda – Idi Amin's staying power amounted to something more than just a freakish run of luck. The British, like the French, also laughed – and they also supplied the goods. Amin's genial obliviousness to what is sometimes called civilised opinion aroused admiration. He echoed needs and instincts to which it is not always easy to give names, but which are nonetheless real for all that. For many blacks, this one-time President of the Organisation of African Unity became something of an alter ego. And this was so not only in Africa. I have met devotees of his as far afield as the Caribbean and the United States. For such as these, the relentless ruination of Uganda – the breakdown of water supplies, the decay of roads and hospitals – was neither here nor there. Economic indices were of no special interest to his admirers. Amin, a primal figure, offered release to pent-up emotions and fantasies; he was able to transform himself and his sinister buffoonery into an intensely experienced spectator sport.

The examples derived from Africa could be piled one on top the other. Still, it is far from my intention to suggest that Africa monopolises the grotesque. Resùrgent – one might also say insurgent – Islam has provided us with another contemporary evolution of behaviour that seems to repudiate conventional interpretations of rationality, to obey standards other than those subscribed to by development economics. Limbs are being amputated in many parts of the Muslim world in the pursuit of Islamic justice and righteousness. The holy war – the jihad – has come right back into fashion.

I was in Iran when the Shah's 'White Revolution' was coming to its end. Now there was nothing intrinsically wrong with the Shah's ambitions for his country. One might argue with the details – the use of torture and so on – but not with the overall intention. Who would criticise agricultural reform? industrialisation? technical training? the attempted reassertion of Iran's long-dormant power and influence? Iran, with its long and glorious past, had every reason to cradle a grandiloquent set of expectations about its destiny. Up to a point, with Persepolis providing the background, one could even sympathise with the Shah's Napoleonic vision of himself. National saviours do tend to have their little ways. The Shah, however exotic he might occasionally appear to be, however archaic the symbolisms he exploited (the Iranian calendar, for example, included dim antiquity in its sweep)

... the Shah was – finally – a comprehensible figure. This Light of the Aryans, this King of Kings, to use only two of his pseudonyms, was tied to the theories and hopes spawned by development economics. Not so the adversaries with whom he had to contend. The messianic mullahs who would bring his throne toppling down had never read an economics text-book and had no wish to read one. I remember the mosque I visited on the outskirts of Teheran one afternoon. Within its precincts, as if in deliberate defiance of the White Revolution supposed to be going on outside, were crowds of black-robed, black-veiled women, their eyes barely registering the existence of the external world. Some were crouched against the walls; others were prostrated in attitudes of devotional ecstasy. Today, their sons and brothers and husbands, holy warriors courting martyrdom on the battle-fields of the Persian Gulf, are dying by the hundred. In the gardens of Paradise, who needs filtered water, good roads, well-equipped hospitals?

What I am trying to show is that a Third World does not exist as such, that it has no collective and consistent identity except in the newspapers and amid the pomp and splendour of international conferences. Human beings don't come conveniently packaged in oven-ready, Identikit format. Islamic resurgence is one thing; the excesses of Idi Amin are another; a Marxist coup d'état in Grenada is yet another. A Sri Lankan massacre is a Sri Lankan massacre – nobody else's. It is not some vague Third World happening to be fitted into the off-the-peg categories manufactured by the Third World ideological rag-trade. Matters have indeed reached a ridiculous pass. The other day I was looking at a biography, written by a French scholar, of one of the most illustrious philosophers of the Muslim world. The man about whom the French scholar was writing lived in the fourteenth century – a period of cultural splendour for Islam. The book is worth a little quotation. The thought of this fourteenth-century philosopher, he tells us, 'can now be seen as a major contribution to the study of the underlying causes of underdevelopment'. Mind you, he adds, the analysis has to be tackled with care – if only because, in the fourteenth century, Islamic North Africa could not be remotely regarded as underdeveloped. The blurb is less restrained. The book, it says, concerns 'the birth of history and the past of the Third World'. Well ... well ... There is no hiding from this Third World business. Down the ages we clank about like felons. Would the Grenadian be pleased to know that he has his Third World roots in the Islamic North Africa of six hundred years ago? That would be a most intriguing self-discovery for him.

The longer I live, the more convinced I become that one of the greatest honours we can confer on other people is to see them as they are; to recognise not only that they exist but that they exist in specific ways and have specific realities. Clearly, it's harder than you might think to do that. If a clever French scholar can't manage it – what hope is there for the rest of us? I am reliably informed that in order to understand the sectarian killings in Northern Ireland one should become acquainted with Irish history and the sentiments to which its convolutions have given rise. That sounds reasonable enough to me; though the same man who gave me that advice looked somewhat shocked when I made mention of Sri Lanka. 'But that's the Third World,' he said. What is true for Ireland should also be true for Sri Lanka and everywhere else. Why have these double standards? We must cast off the rag-trade mythologies with which we clothe our perceptions of mental and spiritual worlds unfamiliar to us. It is said that when the Jesuits first went to China they were appalled by Buddhist rites. They were appalled because they were struck by certain superficial resemblances these bore to certain of the rites of the Roman Church. They concluded that Buddhism was the work of the Devil. The Third World ideologues, clutching their Marxist texts, detecting devilish parallels between Islamic North Africa of the Middle Ages and Grenada, remind me of those early Jesuit missionaries.

The idea of a Third World, despite its congenial simplicity, is too shadowy to be of any use. When, for instance, India is casually included in the unholy brood, what are we really attempting to say? That India is a hot country with many poor people? But the same India has launched satellites, has atomic power-stations, has sophisticated research establishments. It is an old and complex civilisation with old and complex problems. All poverty may look alike from a comfortable arm-chair, may seem susceptible to the same remedies. Nothing could be further from the truth. Poverty is even more varied in its causes and manifestations than wealth. Chinese and Indian poverty are not the same. What will work in omnivorous, centralised China will not work in fastidious, centrifugal India: neurotic, Brahminical sensibilities are very, very different from those engendered by a Mandarin bureaucratic tradition. The Third World is an artificial construction of the West – an ideological Empire on which the sun is always setting. What images come to mind when we think of it? Sun-burnt aid-workers telling television interviewers how civilly they have been treated by their guerrilla captors . . . tempestuous confrontations with the International Monetary Fund . . . here a modest irrigation scheme . . . over there a windmill . . . down the road a tiny medical dispensary of unplastered brick, hailed as a triumph for the principle of self-help . . . and, subliminally, those slow-moving files of refugees in stony landscapes, those immobile babes-in-arms with flies clustered round closed eyes. I am not denying that people need windmills and village dispensaries and all the rest. What I do deny is that these needs adequately sum up the human condition of three-quarters of mankind.

It is nice, I admit, to possess a euphemism for backwardness and – perhaps – for blackness. But, then, there are already so many of those knocking around. Of all the terms available to us – 'underdeveloped', 'developing', 'less developed' and so on – the idea of a Third World is the one least confined by reality and the most promiscuous in the political temptations to which it gives rise. The Caribbean – where, incidentally, I was born – provides us with rich case histories of its harmful effects. There, the discovery of Third World status had, despite the ritualistic noises that were made, comparatively little to do with economic deprivation pure and simple. Its appeal was more visceral. The idea was swiftly harnessed to racial assertion and militancy. In the Caribbean, being Third World meant being *Black*. To be Black was to be *Oppressed:* to be a constantly hurting casualty of the twin evils of slavery and colonialism. A new identity capable of expressing all this had to be found. One of the more harmless affectations was the changing of names. Some turned to Africa for inspiration, some to Islam. Unhappily, not all the transformations were so harmless. In Trinidad the Army fell under the spell of American Black Power ideology and mutinied. Guyana's black supremacist government began to contribute modest handouts to Africa's guerrilla armies. It was in Guyana too, let us not forget, that Third Worldhood was to attain one of its more gory climaxes when, at Jones-town, nearly a thousand mainly black refugees from the United States were half forced/half-persuaded by their revo-lutionary minders to swallow a cyanide-laced cocktail and so demonstrate their defiance of fascism.

But most curious, in a way, were the repercussions in Jamaica. There, the Third World – Blackness – found unex-pected fulfilments in the Rastafarian cult which, among its other articles of faith, preaches the divinity of the Ethiopian Emperor and a return to Africa. Under its influence – spread largely by its reggae music – this quasi-religion, so indulgent to marijuana, was to become the opiate of the masses throughout the Caribbean – and beyond. There are now Africans in Africa who want – if, that is, we take their hairstyle at face value – to go back to Africa. In Australia, when I was there last year, I saw youths of Aboriginal descent wearing 'dreadlocks'.

Third Worldhood outspreads its tentacles everywhere. It has come back home to roost – back, I mean, to the First World where it was invented. In London I live not much more than a mile away from a projected centre for the Black Arts – not, I hasten to assure you, to be confounded with satanism and sorcery. With support from the Greater London Council, ideological Blackness threatens to engulf the life of the mind and the imagination. It is now fashionably radical to inform immigrants from India and Pakistan and Cyprus that they too, for the sake of solidarity, must simplify themselves into Blackness. This travesty unites the Far Left and the Far Right.

In the name of the Third World, we madden ourselves with untruth.

The Death of Indira Gandhi

In early June 1984 on the eve of the Indian Army assault on the holiest of Sikh shrines, the Golden Temple in Amritsar, Indira Gandhi spoke to her people. 'India . . .' she said, 'India belongs equally to Hindu and Muslim, Christian and Sikh, Buddhist and Jain, Parsees and others.' The 'India' she invoked was no stranger to violence internal and external in the years since Independence. During those twenty-seven years Hindu-Muslim butchery had remained a recognised blood sport. Caste had contested with caste. Insurrections had broken out in the border states, and Maoist Naxalites had fomented rebellion among the landless in Bengal and Bihar. Wars had been fought with Pakistan and China. And, of course, there had been the terrors of the Emergency, when the rich had made war on the poor. Crisis, more or less pervasive, more or less intense, was a permanent feature of the national life.

Of all the regions of India – with the possible exception of Kashmir – the Punjab is the most evocative. This is not merely because it is the country's richest state, a showpiece of the Green Revolution (lavishly endowed with irrigation canals, tube wells, tractors and fertilisers, Punjab produces, despite its comparatively modest size, well over half of India's food grains); or – even – because of its strategic proximity to the Pakistan border. It is evocative for another reason: because it is central to both the nightmares and qualified triumphs of the Indian national movement. Especially the nightmares. In Delhi, nearly every other middle-aged person you meet has some memory of Partition, that bloody amputation of the province carried out to create Islamic Pakistan. The horror of that period is a living part of folk memory.

You will hear time and again about the refugee trains stacked with mutilated corpses, about houses and books and pictures left behind in Lahore (Oh, Lahore! Lahore!), about the slow rebuilding of shattered lives and careers on the Indian side of the frontier. Punjabi Hindu and Sikh have a common tale to tell, a shared dispossession to remember. In Punjab, independent India paid heavily for its right to exist. More to the point, in the enactment of the Punjabi tragedy, independent India, it could be said, earned through blood and dislocation the *right* to exist. Consequently, the province – its mere name – can acquire in times of stress a fearful resonance. Kerala may go Communist, Assam may go up in flames ... Indians will read their newspapers and shrug. One more crisis. But let deep-seated disturbance tighten its grip on what remains of Punjab – and they become afraid for themselves.

Already partitioned Punjab, true to its communal heritage, had in 1966 been re-partitioned into the states of Haryana, Himachal Pradesh (areas with Hindi-speaking majorities) – and Punjab (Sikh-dominated Punjabi-speaking). Yet, diminished as it was, the name of Punjab retained its resonance. And for five or six years preceding Indira Gandhi's appeal to her countrymen on 2 June 1984, Punjab's distress had been building. Its vehicle was a resurgent Sikh fundamentalism and its dark angel was a semi-literate peasant, Jamail Singh Bhindranwale. He preached hatred of Hindus (he once exhorted young Sikhs to acquire motor cycles and guns and to roam the land slaughtering Hindus) and preached too the idea of Khalistan, the name conferred on the would-be independent state to be ruled by the Sikhs without fear of competition. During that period his assassins rampaged all over the state and beyond its borders. Religious rivals were killed; editors of newspapers who criticised him were killed; railway stations were attacked; buses were hijacked and Hindu passengers singled out for execution. The Sikh 'moderates' did not disown him. Awed by his power, by his talent for cold-blooded murder, they let him flourish. When Indira Gandhi spoke to the nation at least seven hundred people had been killed by terrorists in the Punjab. Bhindranwale had by then installed himself in the Golden Temple and converted it, as Mrs Gandhi had said, into a fortress. Two days after her radio broadcast the Indian Army began its assault on the Golden Temple. The carnage was staggering. It has been estimated (the figure is Rajiv Gandhi's) that some seven hundred Indian soldiers died in the battle and probably as many as three thousand civilians – both terrorists and pilgrims, who had been in the temple on the day the attack began. A sympathy between the two communities going back nearly five hundred years was in ruins.

Five months later, Indira Gandhi, shot down by two of her Sikh bodyguards, lay bleeding to death in the grounds of her Delhi house. The assassination was the signal for Hindus to begin killing Sikhs. A generation before, they had both been killing Muslims. Now they were killing each other. Punjab was once again exacting a heavy price from India.

'Now I know,' Khushwant Singh, the distinguished Sikh writer, said to me, 'what it must have felt like to be a Jew in Nazi Germany.' We were speaking in his Delhi flat. The previous night it had been besieged by marauding *goondas*. He had had to take refuge in the Swedish embassy. He was in an excitable mood. For him, the situation was incredible. 'So many families, Hindu and Sikh, are inter-related by marriage. We have lived together for generations. It doesn't make sense.' It may not have made sense to Khushwant Singh on that evening, but the mobs who were out on the streets of the city represented another and more abiding kind of Indian reality than the secular state of India could muster. The guards who, betraying trust, traitors to their own vocation, had turned on Indira Gandhi and killed her, represented that other reality; so had Bhindranwale and his assassins. The stories were coming in. Out there children were being burnt to death, corpses were being mutilated, houses were being looted; and, they said, the trains coming in from Punjab were stacked with corpses.

*

It was also a death that had prompted my last visit to India. Then it was Indira's heir apparent, her younger son Sanjay, who had suddenly – miraculously – been removed from the scene when his light aircraft had tumbled out of the Delhi sky. By the purest freak India had been given a reprieve from the gangsterism he had threatened to inflict on his country. Even now, I marvel at that intervention. His mother's death was different. It was of India – that India of narrow instincts and loyalties, the India that arrests the evolution of individual consciousness and offers instead the ecstatic fulfilments of blind sectarian passion. *This* death was not to be marvelled at, as predictable in its way as the ritualistic carnage that had ensued. The India that had killed Mahatma Gandhi had now also killed Indira Gandhi. Her murderers, though, were little different in disposition from her idolaters. At the hospital to which she was taken, fist fights had broken out among her followers when the doctors called for blood. What greater honour than to have one's own blood flow into the veins of 'the beloved leader', this expiring incarnation, we were told, of Mother India? 'Indira is India,' they had chorused while she lived, 'and India is Indira.' Their idolatry had proved no less devastating to the secular state than the bullets of her murderers.

On the morning of my arrival a smoky haze hung over the bereaved capital. Khaki-clad soldiers were everywhere, guns at the ready, patrolling the emptiness in the Friday dawn. I stared at the skeletons of burnt-out buses, burnt-out taxis. The still smouldering wreck of an overturned lorry was abandoned on a grassy roundabout. A calm of sorts had descended after a night of riot and pillage and murder. But it was an eerie dawn. Delhi had become a city of rumour and dread. There was talk of the water supply having been poisoned with potassium cyanide, of dead bodies being thrown into reservoirs. The municipality denied this. 'Water,' it said, 'is absolutely fit for drinking.' One had to believe their assurances. Still, it was all a little trying on the nerves. So was that other rumour about commando units of Sikhs making their way toward the capital from Punjab. This too turned out to be untrue.

In Teen Murti, Nehru's prime ministerial mansion where Indira Gandhi had lived as a young woman, she now lay in state, watched over by the chiefs of the army, the navy and the air force. Her surviving son and successor, Rajiv, most reluctant of princes, stood nearby, gazing at the embalmed, flower-bedecked body. Pundits chanted and droned the sacred texts of the Hindu canon. In death, she seemed no less imposing and powerful a presence than she had been in life. Outside, through the arches of the porch, her people filed by hour after hour, making small offerings of marigolds, shouting slogans, repeating her name as if it were a mantra. The loss of the 'beloved leader' was described by some as 'an unparalleled tragic event in the history of the world'. It was said that she had been the symbol of Young India, of modern India, and would remain the symbol of Future India. No hyperbole was spared for the 'Joan of Arc' of the Indian people. For Yasser Arafat her death was 'a loss for all the freedom fighters'. The Nicaraguan people, according to their country's representative, had lost a dear friend. So had Guyana; so, surprisingly enough, had Uganda – certainly, President Obote and his twenty-four delegates to the funeral seemed to bear testimony to a magnitude of grief no other state could match. The world paid its homage to her, and on the whole Indian self-esteem was highly gratified. Her death and the response to it provided an opportunity for India to assess and relish the international status she had conferred on her country.

Late that Friday evening I risked the journey along Delhi's misty avenues, largely deserted except for patrolling soldiery and roaming army trucks, to Teen Murti. The crowd, held at bay by the curfew, was modest. The autumnal night was sweetened by the odours of dust and smoke and dung. The face on the bier was waxen, a glistening mask of death. Beside the body, an air-conditioner hummed. A group of roughly dressed men and women, pushing before me, made their obeisances to the effigy, bowing their heads, bringing their palms together in the Hindu gesture of respect and reverence. It occurred to me that they were Harijans. I tried to imagine what she had represented to them. In her best moments she must, in their eyes, have seemed to transcend – to be outside and above – the cruel oppression of a Hindu society that had condemned them to nothingness. Certainly, she had been dependent on their votes – just as she had depended on the votes of another significant minority, the Muslims. Secularism, however much an ideal it may be, also has its pragmatic side.

Still, it remains true that no other major figure in contemporary Indian politics had approached her national stature, had come so close to embodying the elusive and perhaps ultimately illusory vision of a secular state which Nehru had laid down as the path to be followed by India. Indira Gandhi, however, was no Koh-I-Noor but a deeply flawed diamond. This 'democrat' – and in some senses I suppose she was that – cannibalised from within the Congress party she had inherited from her father, transforming it into an instrument of her own personal (dynastic) rule; this 'champion of the poor' had presided over an Emergency that had used all the powers of the state against the powerless; and this 'secularist' towards the end had played communal politics in the Punjab and so had brought the Indian union to one of the greatest crises it has ever known. The vices of India tended to mirror the vices of Indira. Maybe that is how we should understand the phrase that Indira was India and India was Indira.

*

That Hindus and Sikhs should now be massacring each other in the Punjab and elsewhere certainly – on the face of it, at any rate – defies reason and (to a lesser extent) disfigures history. The breakdown is a tragic example of the fissiparous tendencies inherent in a country communal by instinct and training. Sikhism, founded by Guru Nanak in the sixteenth century, was, like Buddhism and Jainism before it, a revolt against Brahminical domination and the divisions of caste. Nanak, proclaiming the unity and formlessness of God, also forbade idolatry. Yet the Sikhs, as Khushwant Singh has written, had no particular difficulty in regarding themselves as the 'militant wing of Hinduism'. The enemy as originally perceived was the Muslim in all the various manifestations he has assumed in India – Mogul, Afghan, Pathan . . . Even the theological differences that marked off Sikhism from the parent body did not create barriers to continuing communion between the two. Ranjit Singh, the great Sikh warrior, undertook pilgrimages to the holy places of the Hindus and banned the slaughter of cattle. There was a very porous wall between the two communities. Intermarriage was common. Often elder sons of Hindu families were turned into Sikhs. The holy book of the latter, the Granth Sahib, would be read in Hindu households. It took time for theological divergence to develop into loyalties and rivalries more communal than religious in character. India being India, maybe that development was inevitable. The subcontinent has rarely been able to articulate grievance and ambition other than in a communal fashion. God may be one and formless. Not so his worshippers: they soon learn to cherish their distinctiveness.

It was the British who in their preferential policies of recruitment to the army first sowed the seeds of Sikh chauvinism. Later on, in the early decades of this century, this was further pandered to by the establishment of separate electoral rolls and electorates. These tendencies began to be indigenously aggravated by the revivalist – 'purifying' – movements that appeared among both Hindus and Sikhs. For the Sikhs it came in the guise of the Gurdwara reform movement. This in essence sought to establish overall community control of Sikh temples (*gurdwaras*) and so reserve to themselves the privileges of appointment and administration alienated to British officialdom. Gandhi was all praise. 'India,' he wrote in the 1920s, 'is watching with eager expectation this religious manifestation among the Sikhs. They will without a shadow of doubt solve their own [problem] . . . and assist in solving India's problem.' Nehru, on the other hand, was critical of both revivalist Sikh and Hindu self-assertion. The Sikhs in due course won their battle for control of the temples with the passage of the Gurdwara Act in 1925. Then as later their relationship to the nationalist movement was ambivalent. Introspective, absorbed in the urges created by increasing awareness of their own 'identity', they formed alliances with the nationalist movement which were nearly always tactical, aimed at promoting some end peculiarly their own. This ambivalence they took with them into independent India.

Partition having cordoned off the Sikhs from the Islamic threat, they were now free to devote their full attention to the Hindu threat. In 1966 Indira Gandhi caved in to the agitation for a separate Punjabi-speaking state. The concession solved nothing. Trouble arose over the transfer of Chandigarh, the capital of post-Partition Punjab, to the new state of Hariyana. Four years later, Mrs Gandhi also gave way on the Chandigarh question, but on the condition that certain districts be handed over to Hariyana in compensation. The Akali Dal (the main Sikh political party) objected and went even further, demanding that Sikh-populated areas in Rajasthan and Himachal Pradesh be handed over to them. In 1973 the Akalis passed the Anandpur Sahib resolution. This called for Amritsar to be declared a holy city and the sale of tobacco, liquor and meat to be forbidden inside the walled city. The government said there were no holy cities in India. All-India Radio, the resolution suggested, should transmit daily readings from the Holy Book. Sikhs were to be allowed to wear *kirpans* (daggers) when travelling by air. The Akalis accused Rajasthan of having been given too large a share of the region's water resources – they wanted some of it to be given back. 'Centre-state' relations, they proposed, should be restructured to include only the management of defence, foreign affairs, post and telegraph, currency and railways. By 1981, another version of the resolution was in circulation. This demanded an autonomous region to be created in northern India in which the Sikhs would be constitutionally recognised as being of 'primary and special importance'. Khalistan was creeping out of the shadows.

Abroad there had also been stirrings. In September 1971

Dr Jagjit Singh Chauhan announced in London the birth of Khalistan. He issued passports, stamps and currency. His own passport was revoked by the Indian government. In 1978 an organisation calling itself the Dal Khalsa appeared on the scene. An Indian government White Paper released early in 1984 referred to its founder as 'a pro-Naxalite leader of Birmingham'. This group tried to show it meant business by hijacking an Indian Airlines aircraft in 1981 and ordering it to Lahore. Vancouver was another fertile field for Sikh militants. The talk over there was of power only growing from the barrel of a gun, of suicide missions. These organisations, however they might differ ideologically, all had one strain in common: they were devoted to the cult of violence. Back in the Punjab even the 'moderate' Akali leaders, fearful of Bhindranwale's influence, were falling prey to the fundamentalist mania. Their new cry was for a separate personal law for the Sikhs. This among other things would forbid divorce and the ownership of land by women. Naxalism, fundamentalism, 'moderation' – they were becoming indistinguishable in the chaos enveloping Punjab.

The White Paper responded with a touch of desperation. 'The Indian people,' it is written there, 'constitute one nation. India has expressed her civilisation over the ages, her strong underlying unity in the midst of diversity.'

Secular India was fighting for its life.

*

'My emotions,' Khushwant Singh said, 'are far more Indian than Sikh.' But what, I wondered aloud, was an Indian? Most of the usual categories and tests of nationhood – race, religion, language – did not apply. 'I suppose,' Singh said, 'I mean a certain consciousness of India's frontiers, a geographical consciousness.' He smiled. 'And, there is the river, the Ganges. That is very important.' Others to whom I put the question also invoked the river. It was always there, meandering subliminally through the psyche of the subcontinent. I was sceptical. Did it meander through the psyche of the Muslim? Perhaps, it was conceded, the ancestral allure of the river was weaker in that 'section'. But it was still there. For, after all, what was the heritage of most of India's Muslims? What had they been before the act of conversion? Few had escaped the influence of those brown, silt-laden waters. Was it in me? 'It is there,' I was told, 'it has to be there. You too belong to us, though you may not know it.' I permitted myself a burst of uneasy laughter. 'You must not worry,' a kind man murmured, placing his hand on my shoulder, 'India exists. It may be hard to say why it exists in words, but it does. It lives in all of us, our hearts beat in time with it.' Apparently, irreconcilable diversity was *maya* – illusion. I realised suddenly that the doctrines of Karl Marx were a kind of Hinduism, easily absorbed, easily adapted by the traditions and teachings of the ancient religions. 'All objective reality,' a noted Indian student of communalism has written, 'is grasped through its cognition by the human mind. But not all human thought, consciousness or ideology are equally valid reflections or cognitions of reality. This means that individuals are not aware of their objective reality, though they are aware of their immediate empirical reality.' I think I understand what he is trying to say: that communalism is itself one of the forms of illusion; that the communalist is a victim of false consciousness or, in other words, of *maya*. What a perfect Hindu Marx would have made.

On the day following the cremation of the Prime Minister, I went to Rajghat, the cremation ground of the high and mighty of independent India. There, I visited the *samadhi* of another assassinated leader, Mahatma Gandhi. Pilgrims stood before the slab of black marble heaped with offerings of flowers. They prayed and offered bunches of marigolds. From the top of the grassy knoll that protects the Mahatma's cremation site I looked past the *samadhi* of Indira Gandhi to that of her father, hidden among trees. Not far away was the *samadhi* of his grandson, Sanjay. The Mahatma, Nehru, Sanjay, Indira: each had offered a different vision of India and each had failed. Standing on that grassy knoll, looking out towards the sacred river, one had to grieve for Hindustan.

India and the Nehrus

No one interested in the twentieth-century history of the Indian subcontinent can contemplate its dramas without the accompanying sensations of disquiet and distaste – and even, on occasion, of outright revulsion. The plot, beginning with the struggles of the nationalist movement, is a complex and devious one, a spider's web of often incompatible ideals (Gandhi and Nehru may have been guru and disciple but they also represented quite different images of Indian destiny), hostile interests and confusions of motive. Towards the end (which, for the sake of convenience, we might say comes with the coronation of Rajiv Gandhi), the ideals have disappeared altogether. All that survives are the interests – which have become more naked; and the emotions to which they give rise – which have become more crude. How did it happen that the Gandhi-Nehru legacy decayed into the shabbiest idolatry of family? How was it that India – a country, despite all its poverty and squalor, with a substantial industrial base, powerful armed forces, a sophisticated Civil Service, a well-educated middle-class – ... how was it that India manoeuvred itself into the voodoo politics of Mama and Baby Docs?

I shall take a scene or two from what now passes for political life in India. Towards the end of 1983, Tariq Ali was present at a session of the All India Congress Committee, one of the manifestations of the ruling party.* It should have been a glittering occasion. Present were emissaries from East Germany, Tanzania, France, the Soviet Union. Indira

*The Nehrus and the Gandhis: An Indian Dynasty
Tariq Ali, Chatto and Windus/Picador 1985.

53

Gandhi and her heir apparent, Rajiv, presided. Rajiv, so far as our information goes, had been perfectly content piloting the aircraft of Indian Airlines, the internal carrier. There is no known reason to doubt that he would have gone on doing so but for the sudden death, in 1980, of his younger brother, Sanjay. Cruelly robbed of one heir apparent, Indira Gandhi reached out for the only other available. It takes years of training, I am told, to qualify as an airline pilot. But, it seems, nothing of the sort is required to become the leader of eight hundred million Indians.

'The Congress session,' Tariq Ali tells us, 'was a one-family show . . . Sitting on the floor of the wooden platform were Indira Gandhi and Rajiv, surrounded by provincial leaders. In the audience were delegates from Congress branches in the country as a whole. "Delegate" is perhaps a euphemism. They seemed like people picked up on the street and promised a good time . . . Some of them were constantly being rescued from police cells and brothels.' They chanted slogans ('Who is the leader of our nation?' 'Rajiv Gandhi!') when called on to do so by their cheer-leaders. Only Indira and Rajiv could command their attention and deference. When other speakers tried to address them, the rabble grew noisily restive and drifted away from the hall in droves. The Prime Minister, mindful of the presence of her distinguished overseas guests, was vexed, becoming especially so when it was the turn of her most prominent guest (a member of the Central Committee of the Communist Party of the Soviet Union) to speak.

In desperation, she rose to her feet. 'Look here,' she appealed, resorting to the privacy of Hindi, ' . . . it looks very bad to foreigners when you all leave after I have spoken. Sit down! You near the door, sit down! . . .' It is possible that Tariq Ali has embellished the scene; that he has exaggerated the infantilism. Nevertheless, his description rings true. It is of a piece with the essentially personal and devotional nature of political allegiance in India. Indira Gandhi ought not to have been so discountenanced by the behaviour of her admirers. She had raised no objections when it was proclaimed that 'India is Indira and Indira is India'. If that were indeed so, why should time be wasted listening to anyone else? Congress, as a party, was pure façade; no more than a front organisation for Indira Gandhi and her family. Everybody knew that.

Politics as such – the battle of parties, the conflict of ideologies – had virtually ceased to exist. In that debased atmosphere a quarrel between mother-in-law and daughter-in-law automatically acquired vibrant public significance. After the death of Sanjay, it came to light that his widow, Maneka – never too enamoured of her brother-in-law Rajiv and his Italian wife – was reacting badly to her sudden eclipse and the rapid elevation of her rivals. Whether the disaffected Maneka was expelled or expelled herself from the house of the Gandhis remains obscure. However it was, she lost her resident status. Not everybody who falls out with their mother-in-law responds to the challenge by forming a political party. Maneka did. One morning eight hundred million Indians woke up to discover that their political choice had been enriched by the birth of the Rashtriya Sanjay Manch – the National Sanjay Organisation.

Her party, Maneka declared, would fight for socialism, democracy and secularism; a trinity of aspiration, as Tariq Ali remarks, not usually associated with Sanjay Gandhi. Maneka fought an election against Rajiv. Socialism, democracy and secularism featured little in her campaign. Tariq Ali sums it up well. 'Maneka's main angle at political rallies was to present herself to the poor peasants as a wronged widow, cast out on to the streets by a tyrannical mother-in-law and under the cold eyes of her late husband's cruel elder brother and his foreign wife.'

Politically, India seems to have gone full circle, to have regressed to the shallow but deadly intricacies of the Moghul court on the eve of the British conquest. Is it too fanciful to suggest that one can already discern the dim outlines of future civil wars? The dramatis personae exist – one doesn't have to invent them. Maneka has her little princeling, Feroze; and Rajiv has his Rahul. The dynasticism which, to some, has seemed a blessing, offering India stability and continuity, could become a rather messy business if the claimants to the inheritance continue to multiply. Whatever its successes under the benign guidance of 'Captain Rajiv', the intrinsically capricious character of the dynastic principle will ultimately subvert the too cheaply acquired illusions of stability and continuity. It is a papering over of the cracks that have developed in the foundations of Nehru's 'secular' state. Today, India may embrace the civilised Rajiv; but only yesterday it was recoiling in terror from Sanjay and the demons he had threatened to unleash.

Yet, when we turn our attention away from the Congress Party, when we survey the Indian landscape in search of an alternative, what do we see? We see factionalised Marxist sects not obviously anointed with any conviction of their revolutionary destiny; narrowly based 'chauvinist' movements like the Sikh Akali Dal (Party of Immortals) in the Punjab; in the 'anti-Aryan' South, regional alliances with a purely regional appeal; and we see too, through a polluted mist, those discredited, disgruntled gerontocrats, the Congress 'Old Guard', manoeuvred into the borderlands by the palace coup Indira Gandhi had engineered in 1969 to secure her ascendancy after the death of the ephemeral Lal Bahadur Shastri.

These, roughly speaking, were the men who, in 1977, were to be given a second chance by the Indian people, emerging triumphant from the post-Emergency General Election which had swept away Indira and Sanjay. The failure of their jerry-built Janata (People) coalition went deeper than mere popular disenchantment with the disconcerting eccentricities of a urine-drinking Prime Minister; went deeper than the gross corruption that accompanied the urine-drinking – Indians, after all, were inured to corruption; went deeper – even – than the absurdities: the Minister of Health, for example, didn't believe in modern medical practices. Mutilated by the cut-throat ambitions of the leading protagonists who shamelessly warred with each other, the Coalition vandalised the fragile fabric of Indian democracy. Its sordid,

self-inflicted suttee not only prepared the way for the return
of Indira Gandhi and the feared Sanjay but signalled a
surrender to the dynastic principle. If Nehruian democracy
was to be raped, who better to do the ravishing than the
descendants of Nehru? They might even do it with some
style. And, maybe, some sort of rape had always been inevitable. How do you govern and hold together a country that
defies the very idea of nationality? Nearly forty years after
the coming of Independence and the secular state the most
fundamental questions persist.

'What is Mother India?' Jawaharlal Nehru had asked one
of his audiences some years before the attainment of Independence. His listeners, until that moment ebullient, fell
uneasily silent. In India, nearly everything conspires towards
fragmentation. The challenge to the unity of India comes not
from without but from within. The specific evolutions of
history, religion, language, castes, subcastes, sub-subcastes –
nearly everything tends to divisiveness. In the poorest and
most squalid of villages, communities will isolate themselves
from one another. Some years ago, while travelling in Maha-
rashtra, I visited such a village. It was a stricken place, barely
able to coax one crop of rice a year from the stony soil,
inhabited by low-caste Hindus and Untouchables. Not many
years before, the Untouchables had converted en masse to
Buddhism: others seek salvation by embracing Christianity
or Islam.

Conversion had made little difference to their condition.
Relations between the two groups in the village were no less
strained than they had been formerly. The 'Buddhists' – to
take just a couple of examples – could not draw water from
the same well as the Hindus and had to locate their huts at
a discreet distance. They were all, Hindu and Buddhist alike,
hopelessly destitute, hopelessly separate – and all citizens of
the Indian republic. In any of the neighbouring villages,
these same low-caste Hindus might find themselves similarly
discommoded and reviled by those adjudged their superiors.
In India, degradation and sublimity are subject to the most
delicate shadings. Caste maintains and defines a sense of

self that might otherwise disintegrate into nothingness. It is contagious, infiltrating its sensibilities even where it is formally denied. Neither Indian Christianity, nor Islam – nor Buddhism – has been immune to the infection. Add to caste the other major lines of fracture randomly listed and the question, 'What does Mother India mean to *you?*' assumes alarmingly chaotic implications. When meditated upon, the 'India' invoked by nationalist fervour begins to lose its solidity, melting away into spectral abstraction. Hence, perhaps, the silence that fell when Nehru asked his question.

There is another equally pertinent version of the question: what did Mother India mean to Jawaharlal Nehru? One way of trying to answer this is to consider the background of the man. The Nehrus, interestingly enough, had their ancestral roots in Kashmir, a region peripheral to the main currents of Indian life; and, with its Muslim majority, still squabbled over by India and Pakistan. It is possible that this inherited marginality allowed Nehru to distance himself from the constrictions of the subcontinent's cellular mosaic and to see a 'whole' where a whole may never have existed; or, at any rate, not existed in the sense premissed by nationalist fervour.

Although he never actually lived there – the Nehrus migrated to Delhi in the early eighteenth century – the picture-book romance of Kashmir, its snows, its lakes, its flowered meadows, did always remain with him, colouring his dreams. How subliminally un-Indian the images bequeathed by Kashmir! It smuggled into his perceptions the poetic licence to which the privileged quasi-outsider is always vulnerable. Jawaharlal himself was born in Allahabad, a city on the confluence of the sacred rivers, Ganges and Yamuna. The Nehrus, Brahmins of impeccable quality, were aristocrats. British India, one imagines, could have furnished few better examples of adaptation and assimilation.

Motilal Nehru (Jawaharlal's father), a prosperous lawyer, an ostentatious Anglophile, lived in the grand Victorian manner. One of his son's earliest memories was of his father, warmed by claret, laughing resonantly at the dinner table. Motilal's house with its terraces, columns and cupolas, its rose garden, swimming pool and croquet lawn – splendours picked out at night by floodlighting – reflected its owner's worldly ease. India in its living reality Jawaharlal would discover only in his maturity. His childhood was sheltered, Motilal hiring an English tutor (albeit a somewhat unconventional one – he was a theosophist) for his son. For his daughters he acquired English governesses. Later, Jawaharlal was sent to Harrow, thus sharing an alma mater with Winston Churchill, the great enemy of Indian independence. But Anglophilia couldn't provide perfect protection. At Harrow Nehru experienced the first twinges of colonial unease and anxiety. 'I was never an exact fit,' he wrote in his autobiography. 'Always I had a feeling that I was not one of them.' In due course he went on to Cambridge where he read geology, chemistry and botany.

Imperial life continued on its measured way. Motilal was delighted when he was summoned to attend the *durbar* of the visiting King-Emperor, George V. This event took place in Delhi in 1911. He ordered his clothes for the occasion from London. The future Prime Minister of India rose with a matter-of-fact aplomb to the demands made on him. 'I suppose,' he wrote to his father from Cambridge, 'you want the ordinary levee dress with sword and everything complete . . . The shoes for the court dress will be made at Knighton's and the gloves at Travelette's . . . Heath's man has managed to fish out your old measures and cast, and he will shape your hats accordingly.'

Motilal, nevertheless, remained sufficiently Indian to want to seek out a suitable bride for his son. Jawaharlal, in response to the threat, fished out his own up-to-date notions on love and marriage. 'There is not an atom of romance,' he countered, 'in the way you are searching out girls for me . . . the very idea is extremely unromantic.' Motilal, though, had his way in the end. On his return to India, Jawaharlal married the Kashmiri Brahmin girl who had been found for him. He was twenty-six; she was sixteen. Somehow his romantic modernity survived this set-back. Its ardours and commitments were transferred to the nationalist battlefield, to his vision of India reborn.

The Nehrus, through all the later generations – Motilal's, Jawaharlal's, Indira's – have been Janus-headed: simultaneously martyrs to the nationalist crusade (the youthful Indira was detained by the British during World War II) and fairly typical embodiments of the colonial yearning for 'cosmopolitan' sophistications, the victims and the beneficiaries of what nowadays is called cultural imperialism. I do not mean to suggest that these tendencies are necessarily discordant. On the contrary. It is no accident that Toussaint L'Ouverture was a pampered house slave. Revolutions are more often than not the step-children of under-privileged cognoscenti. They are the ones who most keenly feel the slings and arrows of outrageous fortune. It is always terrible to realise you are *not* 'one of them'. Cultural imperialism is no bad thing. Many of us could do with more rather than less of it. The Nehrus have had few inhibitions about it. The sicklier members of the family were in and out of Swiss and American sanatoria. Indira – Tariq Ali tells us that her favourite city was Florence – was patchily educated in Swiss and English boarding-schools and spent a couple of inconclusive years at one of Oxford's women's colleges. At a time when it was difficult for Indian students to travel abroad, Indira insisted that her sons should be exceptions. 'I couldn't care less what people say,' she remarked, 'I thought it was necessary for my boys to go to England.'

Westernism – 'phoreigness' as the Indian satirists put it – can assume many disguises. In Indira Gandhi, Nehruian modernity betrays degenerative symptoms. That an English education – and this, note, nearly a generation after the coming of Independence – should still be a 'necessity' for her boys is disturbing: Westernism is slipping into a crude devotion to the phoreign. With Sanjay it slipped further down the scale of values, expressing itself in an obsession with motor-cars, tall buildings with lots of glass, wild ecological fantasies of a verdant India and a savage contempt for his poverty-stunned countrymen. Rajiv (his wife, incidentally, is

Italian) has softened the Sanjayite crassness and talks, instead, of the computer revolution. 'Oh,' said one of his close advisers, a fellow Cambridge graduate, to an interviewer, 'we were the Beatles generation.' Tariq Ali mocks at this admittedly curious avowal. A century ago his equivalents in Calcutta would have been discussing Jeremy Bentham and John Stuart Mill. Only in Jawaharlal Nehru, conspicuously the most erudite, cultured and gifted of the clan, did the emphatic Westernising strain in the Nehrus escape caricature and bear its noblest fruit.

The fruit was a noble one – and yet, it has soured and grown bitter. Nehru's romanticism coexisted with a no less powerful rationalism. In fact, the two were linked: dependent on each other, present in each other. His rational romanticism – or, one could say, romantic rationalism – imposed on India the ideal of the secular, non-communal state. This might indeed, in some distant future, be a desirable consummation. But, given the circumstances, few documents are further removed from the human realities they are supposed to regulate than the Constitution of the Republic of India. 'Communalism' has become a byword for all that is bad in India, associated with religious obscurantism, caste degradation and warfare, and the riots and massacres that arise as a consequence. It resurrects, in particular, all the horrors of Partition, of mobs of Muslims, Sikhs and Hindus gathering at railway stations with sword and knife and gun to let loose their blood-lust on the refugee trains transporting the displaced populations.

I do not for a moment gloss over these darknesses. But what is called communalism is not merely the sum of its assorted delinquencies – as Tariq Ali's flawless, text-book socialism would make it out to be. Nehru, unlike Tariq Ali, sensed the arduous and improbable nature of the task he had set himself and imposed on the country. When André Malraux asked this 'un-English English gentleman' (the characterisation is Malraux's) what had been his greatest difficulty since Independence, Nehru mentioned, first of all, 'the creation of a just state by just means'. He paused – then added more concretely: 'Perhaps too creating a secular state in a religious country.'

Communalism, for better or worse, articulates the Indian diversity. Looking down on it from Olympian heights we might wish that it had been otherwise. But it is a brute fact and, however hard we try, there is no running away from it. The Marxists might murmur about false consciousness, but consciousness, false or otherwise, remains consciousness. The divisions and distinctions and traditions bred by centuries of evolution cannot be wished away. The paradox, such as it is, is this. Communalism, while articulating Indian diversity, also expresses the unity of India. Not, obviously, the kind of unity presupposed or required by the 'secular' State, but those broader unities characteristic of an old and intricate civilisation. The old argument about the unity of India comes down to that. India *does* exist; India *is* a unity. However, its existence and its unity belong to a more ancient order of things. Rome began as a State and, as its power increased, became a civilisation. India, more slowly, more undirectedly, accumulated a civilisation and never quite managed to create the patterns of a consistent, self-conscious Statehood. Those, like Tariq Ali, who would abolish 'communalism' by waving the magic wand of class-war and revolution, are, in effect, asking India to abolish itself. That is rather a lot to expect.

For Tariq Ali, despite his irreproachable radicalism, is also one of the victims and beneficiaries of cultural imperialism. How effortlessly he writes about 'peasant spontaneity', 'class demands' and all the rest. When Indira Gandhi's Parsee husband is said to come from a 'petit bourgeois' background, one is overwhelmed by genuine distraction. Marx's man doesn't hesitate to fish out alien measures and casts. Motilal had at least taken the trouble of having his unique dimensions ascertained.

Is there a more fashionable cause around today than the pursuit of 'identity'? All along the way, the secular ideal has had to make concessions to the Indian reality in its various guises. The carving out of states on the basis of language is a major example. So is the 'positive discrimination' practised on behalf of the Untouchables. By what sleight of hand does it become 'chauvinist' – not to say fascist! – for the Hindus of Hindustan to proclaim themselves as such? The secular Indian state, so wary of its minorities, so wracked by the defection of Pakistan, has sacrificed Hindustan as a notion, has refused to accord it legitimacy. Only in the machinations of back-room political calculation and intrigue is it accorded weight. Forced into the shadows, is it any wonder that so many of its manifestations surface out of its murkier depths? Tariq Ali, as the following outburst will reveal, is not in a position to offer remedies. 'The continued strength of religion in the modern world,' he informs us with schoolboy intensity, 'is the most telling indictment of this century ... The members of the Ku Klux Klan in the United States are all firm believers in Christianity.'

Nehru, that un-English English gentleman, was more subtle. In his will he requested that a portion of his ashes be consigned to the Ganges – although, ever mindful of his famous agnosticism, he was careful to disown any apostasy on his part. 'The Ganga,' he wrote, ' ... is the river of India, beloved of her people, round which are intertwined her racial memories ... She has been a symbol of India's age-long culture and civilisation ... I do not wish to cut myself off from the past completely ... I am conscious that I too, like all of us, am a link in that unbroken chain which goes back to the dawn of history ... That chain I would not break, for I treasure it and seek inspiration from it.'

The reinstatement of Hindustan – and I am not advocating the rebirth of some archaic, unhistorical dream world composed of Gandhian self-regulating village republics: no one, including the Hindu, is exempt from the necessities and tribulations of change – might conceivably restore to stationary Hinduism the burden of movement, the burden of moral and intellectual responsibility, which, in part because of secularism, it has relinquished. In that restoration might lie the resolutions which secularism – now even more weakened by the dynastic cult based on the Nehrus – has so far failed to provide.

An Unfinished Journey

The warm night air whipped and eddied through the wide-open windows of the car. At that early hour there was a little other traffic on the road. Occasionally, we passed a cart, bullock-drawn, the circles of its red warning lights gyrating in the darkness; occasionally the driver slammed on the brakes as a dog – or some other animal – loped across the road. Here and there along the verges little groups of men crouched around small fires. Blankly, I stared out at the luke-warm Sri Lankan darkness, at the curving silhouettes of coconut palms, letting the wind flail my face.

*

A lifetime ago, it seemed, I had written these sentences – the first – in my notebook. 'All journeys begin in the same way. All travel is a form of gradual self-extinction.'

I saw myself in the airport at Amsterdam, looking out through plate-glass at a grey mid-morning, at the featureless sky which would soon be swallowing me up. Men and women in navy-blue uniforms were searching for bombs, investigating the foliage of the dutifully decorative plants in their containers, examining ash-trays, frisking the queue shuffling towards the security barrier. The yellow plastic table at which I sat was scorched with cigarette burns. At a neighbouring table English newspapers were being read.

'Police Have Been Superb – Maggie.'

'Tragedy Of Husband With Broken Heart.'

Already I felt myself blurring at the edges.

The woman at the bar said, 'So what part of the world do you come from?' The old question.

Why should she want to know? Of what conceivable use could the information be to her?

'Let's say India,' I replied irritably. The old deception.

As his fingers explored the inner recesses of a fern, one of the security guards laughed resonantly.

Earlier still, there had been the London darkness, the waking out of an uneasy sleep, standing at the kitchen window with a view of the pear tree which was only just coming into blossom, where the birds were only just beginning to stir. Dawn broke with bleak reluctance on the Streatham High Road. As blankly then as now, I had stared at the meagre beginnings of the English countryside. The fields were hazed with mist and the copses were still pools of gloom.

Police Have Been Superb – Maggie.

Tragedy Of Husband With Broken Heart.

I sipped the sweet, tepid beer I had bought. The queue continued to toil through the security barrier. It was the turn of an African woman with two children, one of them a babe in arms. Her slender body was wrapped in a strip of colourful cloth; her cheeks were scarified. A Dutch matron contemplated her. The expression on her face suggested that she was trying to imagine what it was like to be an African woman with scarified cheeks – and was finding the result both incredible and unpleasant. I turned away from them both, looked out at the grey morning and the featureless sky; I laid my notebook across the wounds disfiguring the yellow plastic and wrote: 'All journeys begin in the same way. All travel is a form of gradual self-extinction.'

*

I have been told by more than one person that I have a 'sympathetic' face. 'You are the sort of man I would go up to on the street and ask the way if I was lost,' a girl of congenial temperament once confided to me. Should I have been flattered? I am not so sure. There are more tangible benefits, I suspect, to be derived from having a handsome, 'interesting' or even menacing face. As it is, I have every reason to believe that my friend of congenial temperament was stating a kind of dreary truth: it often seems that I have merely to show myself on any London street for lost strangers of many nationalities to converge upon me and enquire as to their exact whereabouts. A curious circumstance; especially when you take into account the fact that I myself am often as disoriented as they are. Perhaps, when viewed from a suitable distance, perplexity translates itself as sympathy.

But for the traveller like myself – lacking those definite aims, those definite motives, that can be conveniently packaged in the synopses so beloved by publishers and literary agents – this aura of sympathy obviously has its uses. If nothing else, it lends itself to unexpected human contact – and human contact (you never know your luck) can be full of unsuspected fascinations. A journey, one hopes, will become its own justification, will assume patterns, reveal its possibilities – reveal, even, its layers of meaning – as one goes along, trusting to chance, to instinct, to hunch. Journeys undertaken in this spirit – acknowledging, that is, the obscurity of the impulses that have provoked them – resemble a work of the imagination: a piece of fiction, say. Sometimes when we set out to write a novel all we have to begin with are stray, enigmatic images, evanescent scraps of feeling and intuition, which unite to create an intimation of possibility. Our literary labours delve after that possibility and seek to bring it to the surface and give it form. When you start off you do not necessarily know where you are going or why.

I started this section because there suddenly came to mind my alleged possession of a sympathetic face. Why this should come to mind I wasn't sure. But there it was. Now I see that, deviously, it is leading me to the Tamil girl. It is about her I want to write next. She may, for all I know, be taking me nowhere in particular. Still, whatever the case, I want to write about her at this juncture. Does it matter to which specific 'journey' she belongs? I do not think so. She has been waiting in the wings of memory, asking to be let out. Now I shall do so. She may have started talking to me merely because we happened to be sitting next to each other. But, then, she had a choice of neighbours. I will take it for granted that, making note of my sympathetic face, she felt impelled to unburden herself. Below us were interminable plains of greyish cloud; and, below those plains lay the Indian Ocean.

She was, I remember, enveloped in a boldly patterned fur coat, brown and black and white. Twice already the attendants had approached her, suggesting she might be more comfortable without it: it was warm in the crowded cabin. Twice she had resolutely shaken her head, pulling the coat's collar more tightly about her neck, as though afraid it might be forcibly taken from her.

'I do not wish,' she had said in the Gallic tones I had noted with surprise some time before when she had asked for a drink. After the second refusal, she turned towards me, smiling. Her large eyes glowed out of a dark and bony face. 'If I lose it – *très malheureux*. It will be very bad for me. My husband will be angry. They do not understand that.'

I nodded.

Her thin, bejewelled fingers explored and caressed the fur. Again she glanced at me with her large, shining eyes. 'I have been at Paris. With the family of my husband. It is at Paris I buy this coat.'

I nodded.

She continued to play with the fur, her eyes dreamy with the inner contemplation of some vision, though it was not easy to decide whether that vision which so absorbed her was one of sadness or happiness, pleasure or pain. The musky odour of her scent swirled up from her skin, coiling itself about her like another protective sheathing. 'Now I go to Sri Lanka. I go to see my *other* family in Sri Lanka. *Mes oncles, mes tantes* . . .' She might have been talking to herself. 'I walk off this plane in this coat when I get there – to Sri Lanka,' she went on after a short interval of silence, still smiling to herself, still playing with the fur.

'But it will be so hot. You cannot possibly.'

She laughed, volunteering no further comment.

'Where do you live now?'

'I live in Réunion. I am French now. *Française*. No more

68

Sri Lankan.' She fluttered her wrists; she might have been brushing away a pestering fly, a pestering memory. Head angled away from me, she said, 'My husband, he say, "You go. You stay one month with my mother and father at Paris. I give you all these francs. You buy what you like." ' She cupped her palms in demonstration of his generosity.

'Do people wear fur coats in Réunion? Isn't it hot there?' She shrugged.

I asked how long she had lived in Réunion.

'Oh ... (fluttering her wrists) ... *Longtemps*. Many years.' She explained. Her father – he was a dealer in precious stones – had decided to settle there when she was about eight or nine years old. 'Sri Lanka,' she clarified, 'no good for Tamils.' During a riot, their house had been fired, her father beaten up by a mob of rampaging Sinhalese.

'And you?' She turned her glittering eyes on me. 'Are you also a Tamil?'

I did my best. She listened intently. When I had done, she said, 'Brahmin?'.

My response was ambiguous.

'No suppose! No suppose!' She showed signs of agitation. ' Your grandfather Brahmin. Your father Brahmin. You *too* Brahmin.' She jabbed a bejewelled finger against my jacket. '*No* suppose.'

I smiled at her.

'I Brahmin too,' she remarked, losing her vehemence, becoming sombre. She fell quiet for a while. 'You eat the beef?'

I shook my head.

The news appeared to excite her. 'You do not eat the beef? But that is good! Good for your soul, your karma.' Abruptly, her sombreness returned. 'I do not eat the beef either.'

'Good for your soul, your karma,' I responded cheerfully.

'My husband – he don't like.'

'What doesn't he like?'

'He wants me to eat the beef with him, cook the beef for him.' She looked distressed. 'I say to him, "No, no. I am Brahmin." I tell him, "Beef no good for Brahmins." To

69

begin with, he laugh. Now he get angry with me.' She tugged at the collar of her coat, shifted about restlessly on her seat. 'He does not like my tradition. He say, "Stupid tradition. Throw it away in dust-bin." I say, "No, no. Cannot throw away in dust-bin. Tradition is good. Your tradition is good for you and my tradition is good for me." But he does not agree. It makes him angry.'

'Your husband . . .'

She understood at once. '*Oui*. A *blanc*.' She grinned at me, a conspiratorial girl again. 'Shall I tell you how I marry him?'

'Tell me.'

It seemed that on several occasions the Frenchman had seen her strolling about the '*ville*' with her parents. 'You know, I see this man watching me. But I think nothing of it. As a young girl I am *timide* – how do you say *timide?*'

'Shy.'

'*Oui*. I am shy. Very shy.' She paused, considering me. 'You must not think I talk to everybody like this, like I talk to you now.'

I implied that such a suspicion had never entered my head.

'I look at you and I say to myself, "He is a good man. He has *douceur*. I see it in your face . . .'

I stared out across the grey plain of cloud.

'As I say, I see this man watching me, but I think nothing of it. These French people – they're like that.' One day – as she later discovered – he trailed the family party so as to discover where she lived. 'One morning he arrives at our house. I am in the garden, looking at the flowers. He says to me, "Is your Papa at home?" He tell my father, "I want your daughter for my wife." '

'Just like that?'

'Just like that.' She drifted off into reverie.

'And your father,' I prompted. 'What did he do?'

She roused herself. 'My father was not pleased. He say to me, "You know this man?" I say, "No, Papa, I do not know this man. But I have seen this man watching me when we are out on our promenades." And my father – he hit me. He say I not good girl.'

But the Frenchman was an insistent suitor. He came to the house a second, a third, a fourth time.

'What about you? What did you make of it all?'

She smiled as at some distantly perceived object. 'It's like I feel something in my heart for this man.'

'How could you? You hadn't even spoken to him.'

She shrugged. 'You do not always have to speak.'

Her father's threats had no effect. 'He say he send me away from the house, I say, "Send me." He say he beat me, I say, "Beat me." ' A mysterious chemistry (nothing, I was convinced, to do with '*douceur*') was at work and she would have her way. She would marry the man, the utter stranger for whom she felt something in her heart.

Two years previously, in defiance of her father, she had married the Frenchman. Now she was longing for her first child. 'My husband, he say, "I do not like these modern woman. That is why I choose you. You will stay at home. You will have babies." This is the first time he let me go away from him.' Her tone conveyed pride, helplessness, resignation – a fulfilling despair.

'You have no objections?'

'How can I object? It is my karma.' She closed her eyes; she seemed to fall asleep. Soon, though, she was wide awake again. Extracting a vanity case from her handbag, she set to work repairing her lipstick, powdering her chin, her cheeks, her forehead, ogling herself in the little oval mirror.

She simpered at me. 'I am *très coquette*, yes?'

'*Très coquette*,' I agreed.

'I like being *très coquette*. She returned the vanity case to her handbag. 'You know what I would like?'

'Tell me.'

She giggled. 'I would like champagne.' She took hold of my wrist. 'But will you order for me? I pay. But you will order for me, yes?' Her giggles became tinged with anxiety. She reached into her handbag, flourished a handful of francs at me. 'I pay. But you order for me, please. I do not know how. I am so *timide* . . .'

I ordered the champagne for her. She drank it quickly, without obvious enjoyment, as though she was swallowing a prescribed medicine. 'Every night,' she said, 'my husband and I – we drink wine in our house. Every night. I love apéritif also.' She finished the champagne with a grimace. Holding the empty bottle up to her face she swung it back and forth. 'I will show you what else I buy at Paris.' She reached under her seat and dragged out a plastic bag. She exhibited a box of pralines, a collection of furry animals, a colour print of boats on the Seine, a charcoal sketch of herself done by a pavement artist. I admired everything. 'But this,' she exclaimed, 'is my favourite.' She held up for my inspection a pink-faced doll with blue eyes. Its pudgy hands grasped a feeding bottle, the teat of which was clamped to its lips. 'I buy her for me,' she murmured, pressing the doll to her bosom. 'She is my friend. I talk to her. Every night since I buy her she sleeps with me.' She cradled and rocked the doll; she smoothed the coarse, flaxen strands glued to its scalp. 'Now I make her sleep.' They fell asleep together.

During our brief acquaintance, she had slipped into and out of focus. I was alarmed because I felt I understood this bizarre child-woman, overwhelmed by the absurdity of an absurd existence. Like me, the plaything of another ocean, she was compounded out of scraps, this *très coquette*, Brahminical traditionalist who loved apéritifs; who had ceased, even, to possess a language. How could she help but be crazed?

I too was swept away by sleep; a sleep out of which I was startled by a sudden, urgent shaking of my arm.

'*Monsieur* . . . *monsieur* . . .'

I stared without comprehension at a pair of shining eyes.

'Do you speak to God, *monsieur?*' she whispered. 'Do you love Him?'

I was too stupefied to answer coherently.

'I love Him,' she said. 'I speak to Him. He is my friend. He is my only friend.'

I continued to look stupidly at her.

'You too must speak to Him. You too must love Him. Promise me, my Brahmin.'

'I'll try.'

'No try! No try! Speak to Him. Love Him.' Her bejewelled fingers clenched the lapels of my jacket. '*Monsieur – le monde est méchant.*'

*

In the breaking dawn, the empty streets of Colombo looked uninviting and unkempt, the gutters littered with piles of refuse.

I let the wind, brawling through the open windows of the car, batter and flail my face.

*

On my pillow was a card; to the card was affixed a bloom of the white frangipani. 'Welcome,' said the card, 'to Sri Lanka, Pearl of the Indian Ocean.'

*

In the middle of the afternoon I awake, my limbs aching, my head clouded by the uneasy dreams I have been having. I lie there, confused by the hum of the air-conditioner, struggling to piece together the already fading images of the dreams I have been having. I am sitting in a room, all by myself, lined with ranks of school-desks ... before me is an examination paper ... but even as I reach out for the images they vaporise, leaving me only the sensations of disquiet they have aroused; sensations, which, in fact, have prodded me into wakefulness. I look around me in bewilderment. Where am I? Whence that luminousness making the red curtains turn fiery? I jump out of bed, gazing wildly about me, staring at the fiery curtains. Then, on the floor beside the bed, where a pillow has fallen, I see the card and the crushed, wilting bloom of the frangipani. I pick up the card. 'Welcome to Sri

Lanka, Pearl of the Indian Ocean.' Allowing card and flower to slip from my fingers, I start to laugh at the apparition I see reflected in the looking-glass above the dressing table – still garbed, I am suddenly aware, in the clothes in which I have travelled from London; in which, in another life, I had stood at a kitchen window staring out at a pear tree only just coming into flower. Somehow, I summon the energy to shower, shave, dress. On this Sunday afternoon the ornately decorated, high-ceilinged lobby, draped with outsized batiks, is a hive of sociability. Up on a carpeted dais a trio of sari-clad ladies is working its way through a repertoire of sentimental melodies. Tea is being served among the potted palms, the clink of cup on saucer blending amiably with the strains of the sari-clad ensemble.

The afternoon glows yellow beyond the glass doors. Soon I must venture out into it. For the moment, though, overcome by inertia, I linger in the lobby. I know no one in Sri Lanka; I have no introductions to anyone; I have no plan of action. Eventually, I stir myself and move towards the entrance, towards the glowing afternoon. (How fortunate those who can compose synopses and believe in them.)

If journeys always begin in the same way, so too does the 'Third World' – in particular its first manifestations in its capital cities, even more particularly its manifestations in the vicinity of its big hotels. I know more or less what is going to happen as I walk through those glass doors; I know the rituals that will be enacted. Who has made the blueprint? Nobody can say.

Almost immediately, the Man I am expecting appears, detaching himself from a patch of shade. He sidles up because, in this dance, they always 'sidle' up. Do I want to change money? Do I want a girl? Perhaps I want a very young girl? A boy? Hashish, then?

I am heading for Galle Face Green, Colombo's seaside promenade. If my map of the city is accurate it should be no more than ten or fifteen minutes' walk.

Time enough for the rituals of the poor to run their appointed course.

As the Man falls away, returning to his patch of shade, he is replaced by the Beggar Woman With Baby.

'Good, kind sir . . . two rupees . . . only two rupees, good, kind sir.' The bunched fingers jab at the pinched mouth. My heart is stone. 'Milk for the little baby, good, kind sir. You cannot be so hard to the little baby, good, kind sir.' The dwarfish creature presses close against me, trotting along nimbly at my side. Eventually she too drops away.

Her place is taken by the Legless Man With Crutch. When I first catch sight of him, he is leaning against a lamp-post. With practised agility and assurance he plunges into the stream of traffic, dodging this way and that, making for me, his stubbled face fractured by a leer.

Ahead of me, Galle Face Green, a treeless expanse of grass bordered by the foaming ocean, shimmers and trembles in a haze of pink dust. Legless Man With Crutch is not persistent. Family groups stroll along the asphalted path running beside the ocean whose spray, shattering among the rocks, becomes iridescent in the afternoon light. Pairs of lovers sit on the thin grass. Over their heads, colourful kites dip and soar against the cloudless sky. Beyond the arid Green rise the taller buildings of the Fort district, Colombo's business centre. I examine the façade of the Galle Face Hotel bordering one side of the Green and having a fine view of the ocean. Tables and chairs are set out along its shaded, balconied veranda. Ceiling fans revolve in its interior gloom. Its faded, 'colonial' air is alluring, more alluring than the pretentious modernism of the caravanserai from which I have come. A banner above the entrance advertises an art exhibition which will start the following day. On impulse, I go in. There is much activity in the spacious entrance hall. The canvases of the exhibition are being unpacked under the rattling rotations of the ceiling fans. Workmen scurry about, harried by a man of middle-age wearing sandals. I am in luck. 'We have many free rooms,' a melancholy clerk informs me. 'Many, many.' I book myself in.

*

At two o'clock in the afternoon, the bleak, shadeless expanse of the Green was virtually deserted – except for a ragged boy who tried to sell me one of his colourful kites, and a solitary pimp. Neither was too importunate: in the tropics, at two o'clock in the afternoon, who can take himself seriously? Extreme heat, like extreme cold, is conducive to introspection. It was a sadness I remembered from boyhood. The waves breaking among the rocks below the asphalted promenade (I wondered – as a child, did that Tamil girl walk here with her parents?) exuded the odours of sewage; crows swooped through the afternoon emptiness, shadows scything across the grass.

I had not had too good a morning. Now, tired out, shaded by my hat, breathing in the pink dust smoking up in miniature whirlwinds from the scorched grass, I kept my gaze fixed on the distant, welcoming whiteness of the Galle Face Hotel – into which I had moved a couple of days before. First of all, there had been my pilgrimage to the offices of the British Council. They might, I had reasoned, decide to be helpful to a visiting writer. I should have known better. Really I should have known better. But, of course, hope – however battered by experience – springs eternal. I have had my troubles with the Council in various parts of the world. Once, when I was rash enough to mention some of these on a BBC radio programme, the response of the organisation's Public Relations Department had been swift. They had, I was informed, received a number of complaints about me. 'We were glad to hear,' the man from the Public Relations Department went on, 'that you drop in on Council offices when you are overseas, but sorry that you so often go away disappointed with our suggestions for people to meet. We shall try to do better!' Was I, therefore, to be blamed for trying my luck yet again? After all, the man from the Public Relations Department had explicitly denied that his organisation – devoted to the promotion of British culture – disliked writers.

The Council was handsomely housed. Within, the cultural silence was stamped with the chill of efficient air-conditioning. I was directed up carpeted stairs to a slim woman in a sari. Straightaway, I could divine a number of things: that she was preoccupied, that she had no idea what – if anything – should be done about me, that, not to put too fine a point on it, I was wasting my time and she was wasting hers. Dutifully, I stated my extinct hopes.

She looked sad. Trouble was, she said, the Representative was away for a couple of months. Actually, hardly anyone was around. The New Year holidays (she meant the New Year as determined by local traditions) were coming up. There was, in addition, a terrible drought raging throughout the island. All in all, I had arrived at an extremely inopportune moment.

'So, you can do nothing for me.'

Her look of sadness persisted. 'I didn't exactly say that.' With an air of deepening distraction, she reached across the desk for an address book. She murmured to herself as she scanned the pages. 'There's this Goonetileke . . . ah, but he's out of station . . .' She beat a pencil against the edge of the desk. She brightened up marginally. 'Now, there's this fellow . . .'

'What's his name?' I produced my own address book.

'He too is Goonetileke.' Goonetileke No. 2 had just published a massive Sri Lankan bibliography in several volumes. 'He can tell you *everything* you would want to know about Sri Lanka.' Her eyes fixed vacantly on the address book, she went on beating the pencil against the edge of the desk.

I said I wasn't sure I wanted to meet someone like that. My aims were more modest. Couldn't she put me in touch with, say, a lecturer in the English Department at Colombo University?

She stared dully at me. 'Trouble is University's not in session.' She returned her attention to the address book. 'There's this fellow. Head of Department. But he's not at Colombo.' She mentioned a university of which I had never heard.

'What's his name?'

'Goonetileke.'

I stared at her.

'It's quite a common name in Sri Lanka.'

I wrote down the details about Goonetileke No. 3 in my address book.

'Trouble is what with the New Year holidays . . .'

'The Goonetilekes would have all gone back to their homes,' I finished the sentence for her.

She looked at me coldly. Nevertheless, she wrote down my name and my address. 'If I think of anything, I'll call you.'

Our interview was over. I returned downstairs, passed through the deep cultural silence of the library where a scattering of students, defying the New Year festivities and the drought, was absorbed – embalmed – by study. One or two, eyes hypnotically glazed, raised their heads as I went by.

I wandered aimlessly about the crowded, charmless streets of the Fort district. Idle knots of men and boys lounged in the shade under the arcades. The roads were dirty, the buildings peeling and dilapidated. The brassy heat of mid-morning seemed to magnify the din and clatter. Seeking refuge, I entered a bookshop. Within its musty gloom, I found myself witnessing a confrontation between the First and Third worlds. A youthful American, much harassed, soaked with sweat, was holding aloft a guide-book wrapped in cellophane.

'Why can't I remove the wrapper? Why can't I see what's inside?' The American, his voice raised nearly to a shout, was waving the book at the assistant standing behind the counter.

'Cannot,' the assistant replied equably, reaching forward across the counter to take away the book from him. 'It is new book. Cannot remove wrapper.'

Books, I was aware, were like gold dust in Sri Lanka. Those on sale in this shop were, for the most part, locked away like jewels behind glass cabinets. A cursory examination revealed a random and dusty assortment of quaint titles – out-dated European histories, forgotten novels, books on various technical subjects. In addition there was a collection of more up-to-date – but no less randomly selected – paperbacks. It was no surprise that the British Council aroused the reverence it did among the locals.

'How do you expect me to buy a book if I don't know what's inside it?'

The clerk maintained his equability. 'You pay for book, *then* you remove wrapper.'

The American was declining into frenzy. He was almost screaming now. 'You garbage head! What kind of bookshop is this? What kind of goddamned country is this?' He glowered in my direction, swallowing me up in the sweep of his outrage. The assistant had now come out from behind the counter and was circling round his quarry. He lunged at the book, but the American, several inches taller, easily evaded him. 'Do you know what you are?' the American asked him in a tone that teetered on the casually conversational.

The assistant looked up trustingly at his adversary.

'I'll tell you what you are,' the American shrieked. 'You are a pain in the ass. That's what you are. A goddamned pain in the ass.'

Undeterred, the assistant lunged again at the book. Perhaps he had not understood the insult that had been offered him. Perhaps he did not care. The American danced away from him. 'And do you know what this country is?' he shouted, shaking the book in the man's face.

The assistant paused. As before, his face registered interest in the question.

'This country is the arm-pit of the world.'

'Sri Lanka is poor country,' the assistant conceded. 'That is true. Sri Lanka is not rich like your country.'

The American was not mollified by this candid admission. 'It's the goddamned arm-pit of the world,' he stormed on, 'and you are its number one ass-hole.' He tossed the book on the floor and walked out.

The assistant picked up the book, dusted it, scrutinised with sorrow the rents in the cellophane wrapping, attempting to smooth out the mutilations with a finger. He looked at me. 'Cannot now, sir.'

'Cannot now what?'

He tapped his watch. 'If you want book, you come see me later. Not now. Now close for lunch.'

I considered him in some astonishment. 'Do you ever sell anything?' I asked.

'Business is a little slow, sir.'

The Chinese restaurant where I had lunch was obviously popular and none too clean, serviced by a gang of garrulous waiters adorned in food-stained shirts and aprons. I ate sparingly and nervously, avoiding the thumb-printed tumbler of water that had been brought me. Now, walking across the vacated Green, with the taint of sewage rising from the seashore, it was hard not to be apprehensive; not to recall, with rising alarm, the abandon with which carelessly tended hands had soiled my plate, my knife, my fork.

*

How pleasant it was to arrive, still unharmed, at the portals of the Galle Face Hotel. Feeling in need of diversion from my gastric fears, I thought I would take a look at the art exhibition which had started the previous day. The sandalled, middle-aged man, whom I had seen supervising the installation of the canvases, was the only other person present in the hall. He was seated on a low-slung chair, legs crossed, smoking a cigarette. On a table beside him lay a pile of what I assumed to be catalogues. He glanced fleetingly in my direction as I came into the hall and, as quickly, swivelled away, thereby communicating his utter indifference to my presence. This was disconcerting and, for the moment, deterred me from approaching him and asking for a catalogue. The paintings, executed in blurred, muddied colours, were intimations of vaguely human forms. These indistinct, amorphous adumbrations loomed out of canvas after canvas. Their intended profundity was unnerving.

When I had completed the circuit of the hall, I summoned up my courage.

'Are you the artist?'

It cost him an effort to angle his face towards me. Cigarette in hand, he gestured dismissively. 'Artist . . . what is artist?'

'Are you the person who painted these pictures?'

He stubbed out his cigarette, he pulled himself upright. 'The question of *who* is problematical.' He smiled enigmatically. 'Art is matter of spirit. Who is who?'

'I mean are you the person who – physically – painted what I see on these walls?'

He lit another cigarette. I could see his toes waggling in the sandals. 'I am indeed that person.' He blew a perfect smoke ring. 'I am the physical vehicle of those paintings. I claim no more.' His toes waggled.

I sensed a churning in my stomach and was introspectively silent.

'You are looking,' I heard him say, 'at the creation of many years of agony.'

I collapsed into the chair nearest him.

'Agony,' he repeated. 'Years of agony.' He blew another perfect smoke ring.

'Sorry . . . ,' I heard myself say.

'Sorry? What do you mean by sorry?' He spoke without charity.

'I mean . . .' But I had no idea what I meant; my stomach was in rebellion.

He studied me with greater interest. 'You are not from Sri Lanka?'

I explained.

'Ah . . . you must be so kind as to forgive me in that case. I thought . . .' He jiggled his toes, he blew a perfect smoke-ring. 'So we can talk.' He laughed. 'Here in Sri Lanka,' he went on, 'the people do not understand creation. They do not understand art or care for it. I avoid my own people as much as possible. I am polite to them – but distant. Here they're all philistines and barbarians. I have told them so but they do not listen.' His eyes swept along the canvases lining the room. 'Money. It is all money nowadays.' He exhibited disgust. 'Look at them!' He waved his arms towards the door.

'Look at whom?'

He laughed more loudly. 'Exactly! Exactly! Look at *whom* indeed. You do not see all those people fighting to get in the door?' His laughter ceased. 'I don't either. Consider. Apart from you – a foreigner – and me – the artist who has endured years of agony – who else is here?'

'Maybe it's the time of day,' I said, striving to ignore the churning of my stomach.

'The time of day?' He exhibited scorn. 'No, sir. I assure you it's nothing to do with the time of day. You may take my word for that. I know my own people very well. If I were sitting here handing out rupees, they'd all be here. The whole of Colombo would be flocking here.' He waved his arms, lit another cigarette, crossed and uncrossed his legs. 'No . . . it is not the time of day. It is the time we are condemned to live in. A thousand years ago in Sri Lanka we understood creation. Go and see our ancient cities – Anuradhapura, Polonnaruwa. Go and see our old tanks and irrigation canals. We knew how to build then, we knew how to create. But not today. In Sri Lanka we stopped being men a long time ago. You may take my word for that.'

He was too overcome by emotion to go on. Overhead, the ceiling fans whirred and clacked. Out on the empty spaces of the Green, the wind stirred the haze of red dust, bringing with it the odours of sewage.

I rose unsteadily, making what excuses I could for so precipitately ending our conversation and, under his bemused, self-absorbed gaze, fled to the safety of my room.

It was dark in the room when I was startled awake by the pealing of the telephone.

'Mr Goonetileke would like to speak with you,' the telephonist said.

The line was bad and I could barely make out what my caller was attempting to tell me, but I did manage to catch the words 'British Council'.

'Are you the Goonetileke who has just had a book – a bibliography – published?' I shouted.

He shouted back. I picked up the word 'author'.

'You are the author?'

'Yes. The author . . .' But it was impossible to pursue the intricacies of conversation.

We managed to agree that we would meet at his office the following morning.

I went to the window. Twilight had set in. A murmurous crowd paraded on the Green and processed under the blue lamps glowing along the length of the asphalted promenade. In the gathering darkness, the lights of scattered food-stalls shone out brightly. A salmon-coloured sunset washed the western sky, staining the crests of the foaming waves. I stood there, breathing in the air, watching the evaporation of colour from sky and water, listening to the murmur of voices floating up to my window.

There was a knock on my door. The room-boy (he was, of course, not a boy, but a man of somewhat timorous countenance, probably in his late thirties) entered wheeling a trolley and carrying fresh towels draped over a spindly arm. I remained at the window as he bustled about. As a finishing touch, he placed on the slip-case of my pillow a red hibiscus and a chocolate wrapped in gaudy paper.

'You are a friend of the artist gentleman, sir?' His tone was wheedling, uncertain – as sallow as his unhealthily yellow face.

'I met him for the first time today. Why do you ask?'

'He tells me you are a foreigner, that you are from London. Is that so, sir?'

'That is so.' I was not encouraging: room-boys are literary embarrassments – as embarrassing as taxi-drivers. But, alas, both room-boys and taxi-drivers undeniably exist. What can the poor traveller/writer do but occasionally acknowledge that fact? What else can they do but brave the snobberies of their reviewers?

The room-boy hunched his shoulders, he smiled. I recoiled from him a little.

'You like Sri Lanka, sir?'

I was noncommittal. 'What about you? Do you like Sri Lanka?'

'I am not sure, sir.' He laughed a twittering, nervous laugh.

'Why aren't you sure?' I was severe, acutely aware of the literary dilemmas this encounter would raise.

He stared down at the Green on which night had fallen. 'This is violent country, sir. Much hatred, much killing. Sinhalese feel that this is their country. Tamils do not like for Sinhalese to think that. So they hate and kill each other. It is terrible, sir.' Was it my sympathetic face that made him want to talk? Or was it due to my being 'foreign'?

'And what are you? Sinhalese? Tamil?'

'I am none of those, sir. I am Christian. My name is Fernando. A Christian name, sir. My home town is Ratnapura. Have you heard of Ratnapura, sir?'

I said I had.

'Would you like to visit, sir?' As the idea took shape in his head, his meagre body vibrated. 'For me and my family it would be a great honour, sir. It would be very auspicious for us to have you in our house for the New Year.'

My response was guarded. Whatever good fortune it might bring, a visit to a room-boy's family struck me as being the height of foolhardiness.

'Let's discuss it another time.'

His animation lessened. 'Whatever you say, sir.' He readjusted the towels on his arm. 'Are you married, sir?'

He sighed again at my answer. 'I have large family. Many sisters. I look always for husbands for them. In Sri Lanka it is not easy.'

'You were hoping to marry me off to one of them, were you?'

'No, no, sir. Nothing like that. I was hoping the honour of your visit would bring us good luck.'

At that moment there was a commotion on the road outside – stifled shouts, thumps, the sound of stampeding feet. I went to the window. Policemen with batons were running across the Green. Other shadowy figures darted this way and that among the flickering lights of the foodstalls.

'What's happening down there?'

'Police raid, sir. Galle Face Green – too much drugs. As I was saying, sir, Sri Lanka is a terrible place.'

The commotion died away.

'I talk to you another time,' Fernando said. 'Maybe you change your mind. Maybe you come to Ratnapura after all.'

Smiling his sallow, uncertain smile, he wheeled his trolley out of the room and disappeared down the corridor.

*

I sit in an office lined with books and files, overlooking a small garden. Through the open window I can see mango trees, their shiny leaves stirring in the wind. Mr Goonetileke, seated at his desk, is sipping a soft drink; tea has been ordered for me. I treat him with the deference due to a man who has recently brought to fruition a multi-volumed enterprise of scholarly research. But, all the same, my admiration and deference are tinged with muted surprise. Mr Goonetileke doesn't conform to my idea of what a bibliographer ought to look like. He is too young, too vigorous of build; altogether lacking in the austerity I would associate with so fanatical a vocation. It cannot be denied: he is deficient in *gravitas*. He has the demeanour of a successful and secure university lecturer. I sense a wife, children, a pleasant bungalow, regular attendance at conferences abroad. At last a secretary brings my tea.

I smile as I say, 'This may sound a little strange – but I was expecting someone older.'

'Were you? But why?' He wrinkles the corners of his eyes. Nevertheless, he maintains his courteous air.

'You know – one develops images of the people involved in certain occupations. Yours, for instance, brings to mind monastic habits.' I smile again.

'Monastic habits!' Mr Goonetileke seems a little startled by this. With emphatic deliberation, he rests his glass on the desk. 'That is most interesting, most original. If I may be so bold – why did you have that image of me?'

I laugh, uneasy now. 'Because yours, by its very nature, must be such a cloistered occupation. To be candid, I was expecting someone a little older perhaps.'

Mr Goonetileke is at a loss for words. He stares at the restless leaves of the mango trees.

'It's all very silly,' I say.

He turns to me again. 'I am not understanding fully . . .'

'I mean it's silly to expect that a bibliographer will look like . . . well, will look like a bibliographer.'

'I see . . .' Mr Goonetileke leans his elbows on the desk, brings his palms together. I have the feeling that he does not 'see' at all. 'I see . . . but I am still not understanding fully.' He glances around the office, as if suspecting the intrusion of an alien presence.

The terrible truth dawns. 'You are not the bibliographer – the man who knows everything about Sri Lanka?'

'I know a few things about Sri Lanka. But this bibliographer – who is he?'

'A woman at the British Council told me about him.' My tea-cup rattles in its saucer. 'You are not by any chance a Professor of English?'

'I am not that either.' Mr Goonetileke rests his chin on his clasped palms.

'Pardon me for asking. But which Goonetileke are you?'

'You may say I am the Goonetileke involved in development studies.' He smiles, lifting his head, unclasping his fingers.

*

'You ask,' Mr Goonetileke said, permitting a note of condescension to creep into his voice and attitude, 'what distinguishes Sri Lanka from India, what qualifies Sri Lanka to be the unique polity that it is. What makes us, you want to know, something other than another Indian-type state with its usual quota of communal and other problems. Do I paraphrase you accurately?' He leaned back in his chair, he clasped his fingers, he threw back his head and he contemplated the ceiling. An attempt at what might have been a smile caused his cheek muscles to quiver. 'You want me, in other words, to justify our existence as an independent and separate nation-state to you. We have been put in the dock.'

Clearly, I had displeased him. What was also clear was that, as he elaborated his alleged paraphrase, he was discovering just how displeased he really was and rather relishing the sensations it aroused in him. Straightening himself, he looked sardonically at me. We were not, I had quickly realised, to have a conversation as such. The expert in development studies was too steeped in the declamatory traditions of the lecture hall and the pieties of the seminar room to allow himself anything so 'unstructured' as a conversation. I knew I should get nothing of intrinsic value out of him – one rarely does from those who seek sanctuary behind desks and do their talking from within the assurance thus provided.

Mr Goonetileke was a not unfamiliar type. I have met many other touchy mandarins in other poor and touchy countries: men who, at one and the same time, are proud of their cosmopolitan connections and accomplishments and are jealous guardians of the petty nationalisms from which they have benefited. He was, I had managed to elicit, a supporter of the government and its policies, and as a consequence could (officially) be regarded as 'right-wing'. On another occasion, however, I was to listen in some stupefaction to the praises he lavished on the Soviet dictatorship. He was, in his way, a man for all seasons. Like other mandarins of the type, his consummations were enacted on the international conference circuit, finding their physical expression in 'papers' and occasional monographs (he had shown me a few he had composed) laboriously researched in libraries and written up for the occasion. 'I seem to spend half my life in airports,' he had remarked affably. Now he was working on another 'paper' (I forget about what) to provide him with another jargon-laden passport to the splendours of abroad, to all those exotically tinctured bottles of duty-free Dutch liqueurs which, doubtless, he brought home from his travels. Now and again I have taken the trouble to read such papers and monographs. Only in fits and starts do they describe anything recognisable. Generally, the worlds depicted therein can be neither touched, nor seen, nor smelled, nor tasted, nor heard. The practitioners of the art delineate fairy realms of diagnosis, prognostication and prescription beyond the senses. They inhabit a fourth dimension of reality; they make up a Fourth World clamped down like an incubus on the Third one sanctified by our contemporary folklore.

'I must observe,' Mr Goonetileke said, 'that your question is a strange one. I have not been called upon to answer such a query before. However, I will try to oblige you.' He gazed out towards the mango trees.

Where better to start than with Buddhism, the island's dominant religion? True enough the Buddhist doctrines had first seen the light of day on Indian soil. But it was no less true that the religion had died out in India a long time ago, making for itself a new home in Sri Lanka. This reincarnation of Buddhism in Sri Lanka inevitably involved the evolution of significant differences between the island and its subcontinental neighbour. It had meant, above all, that caste in its Indian sense – with all its associated fears of defilement and pollution – did not exist in Sri Lanka. In their mental and spiritual make-up the Sinhalese, as a result of this, represented a different kind of human being.

'You must be aware,' Mr Goonetileke said, 'that Buddhism denies the importance of caste.'

'Theoretically it does,' I said. 'But did it actually work out like that in practice? One could make a comparison with the Communist Manifesto and the socialist states that actually exist.'

Mr Goonetileke threw back his head, contemplating the ceiling. I waited penitently.

Of course he was not denying that caste of a sort did exist in Sri Lanka – one had only to read the marriage columns of the newspapers to discover that. Falling silent, he permitted himself another tremor of condescension.

His reference to the marriage columns of the newspapers was revealing. Was it, I wondered, only through such documentary evidence that he was able to 'discover' and assert the existence of a kind of caste feeling in Sri Lanka? Was he not able to detect its existence in himself, in the patterns and prejudices of his own life, in his own 'mental and spiritual make-up'? He had divorced his life as a professional researcher from that other life he must live as a Sinhalese. They did not connect with each other, occupying quite separate spheres. It was this that made it possible for him to present Buddhist theory as though it were a flawless mirror of social fact. Fine names can be used to justify this counterfeit. 'Objectivity' is one of these. 'Scholarship' is another.

Mr Goonetileke talked on. The applications of caste in Sri Lanka were secular, not religious. Depressed groups like the Untouchables had never existed in the island.

'Among this people,' Robert Knox had written of the Sinhalese towards the end of the seventeenth century, 'there are divers and sundry Casts or degrees of Quality . . .' These categories were not determined by wealth but by descent, by blood. Infringements of these caste boundaries were punishable offences. Whether or not this rigidity can be described as 'secular' is debatable. Knox was no casual, itinerant observer of the Sinhalese scene. A victim of shipwreck on the Ceylonese coast in 1659, Knox, together with several of his comrades, was taken captive by the irascible king of Kandy and held for twenty years in the open prison of the hill country. His book, *An Historical Relation of Ceylon*, is celebrated for its accuracy. There may have been no Untouchables in Ceylon. Yet, as Knox recorded, there did exist a group whose condition bore a perilously close resemblance to theirs. 'There is one sort of People more,' he wrote in the catalogue he gives us of the divers and sundry Casts, ' . . . they are the Beggars: who for their Transgression . . . have by former Kings been made so low and base, that they can be no lower or baser.' So repugnant are they to the other castes, 'they are not permitted to fetch water out of their Wells . . . Neither will any touch them lest they be defiled.' There was one practice which further degraded these 'Beggars' in the eyes of their countrymen: they were beef-eaters. The Sinhalese, however much their manners and customs had been modified by adherence to Buddhism, had not entirely thrown aside all the baggage bequeathed to them by their distant North Indian origins. India also fostered the stress they placed on their 'Aryan' ancestry and accounted – if only by hearsay – for the quasi-racial hatred nurtured against the Dravidian Tamil minority. Nevertheless, the urges of a petty nationalist creed and the pique which it engenders erect barriers against whatever might threaten its self-interested mythologising. Mr Goonetileke was an unabashed beneficiary and servant of a mythology that simplified and distorted the perceptions of the Sinhalese.

I listened to him.

If Sri Lanka, he amplified, had avoided the taint of Untouchability, it had also avoided the oppressions and exactions of a Brahminical priestly caste. 'You must know,' he said, 'that Buddhism forbids the accumulation of personal wealth.' In Sri Lanka, he added, beggary – sanctified by the scriptures – was no shame. The *bhikku* (monk) owned his two robes, his alms-bowl and not much else.

Once more he was offering me an expurgated version of the facts. These self-abnegating *bhikkus* with their two robes and their alms-bowl also had their hierarchies, expressed by different styles of dress and the accoutrements they were permitted. Some bared one shoulder; some bared both; some were allowed the dignity of a talipot-palm leaf as shelter from the sun; others carried umbrellas and yet others were forbidden umbrellas; the colours of robes, as well, were indicative of hierarchical splendour or the lack of it. The different groups carried out their religious offices in separate temples. Intercommunion between these could be difficult.

But didn't the monasteries – I asked – accumulate great wealth? Didn't they come to own vast acreages of land worked free of charge by an obedient peasantry? Couldn't it – hadn't it – been argued that the monasteries had become parasitic institutions? A soft option for hordes of idlers who cloaked their corruptions in piety?

Mr Goonetileke blinked. 'That is a complex issue,' he replied. 'It needs to be properly investigated and analysed.' He waved his hands. 'You know, we do not have all the statistics such a study would require. In their absence we cannot make such definitive statements as you would like.' Leaning back in his chair, he smiled pleasantly, even with a glint of triumph.

I referred to the monkish involvement in worldly affairs, particularly their intervention in the now endemic anti-Tamil (Tamils are not merely Dravidian – they are also Hindu) agitations leading to the riots, massacres, insurrections and 'emergencies' that had scarred the history of Sri Lanka since the coming of Independence.

'Before you were talking of the faraway past,' Mr Goonetileke said. 'Now you take a giant leap to the Buddhist revival.' He laughed. 'Still, I am here to please.'

I was beginning to weary of the man.

Mr Goonetileke clasped together his palms. He was ostentatiously unruffled. 'The Buddhist revival began at about the turn of this century,' he proceeded. It was what he liked to call a cultural resurgence. It marked the birth of modern nationalist feeling in Sri Lanka, their sense of being a 'unique polity'. Annie Besant and her theosophist disciples had played their part. 'You must not forget that they were great admirers of the spirituality of the Eastern cultures.' He picked up from the desk the glass that had held his soft drink, turning it in his fingers this way and that. 'Is there anything wrong with a cultural revival? Why shouldn't we be proud of our culture? Our roots? What is wrong with the Sinhalese wanting their own identity? Why should everybody else have theirs and not us?'

'You talk of "culture" as if it were an item you could pick up from a supermarket shelf and take to the checkout counter. Isn't it a bit more delicate, more elusive, than that?'

'You must understand what violent emotions the language

problem aroused,' he said. 'I do not mean the language problem with the Sinhalese and Tamils. I mean that between Sinhalese and English. The Sinhalese people called English "the sword".'

'Why?'

It was the sword that had been used to cut them off from the higher reaches of attainment. 'What happened in 1971 was instructive. At Colombo University the Sinhalese tried to burn down the library. Why? I will tell you. Because all those books in English symbolised their thwarted hopes.'

'Didn't they also symbolise the cultural shortcomings of the Sinhalese?'

Mr Goonetileke smiled.

'Could the Sinhalese not have asserted their cultural identity, their desire for roots, at the expense of the Tamils?'

Mr Goonetileke turned the glass in his fingers, studying the distorted reflections it returned of the world outside the window. 'That is a complex issue,' he said.

'You lack the statistics to make a definitive statement . . .'

'I agree it is wrong for people to kill each other,' Mr Goonetileke averred. He rested the glass on the desk.

'It is certainly forbidden in the Buddhist texts.'

'That is so,' he concurred without especial irony.

'Then why, in your opinion, do all these terrible things happen in Sri Lanka – and go on happening?'

'The issue is . . .' But Mr Goonetileke had the foresight to stop himself. 'The original phase of aggression has since died out.' He waved his hand. 'Our problem is no longer the majority. The Sinhalese have the kind of state, the kind of polity, they want. Our problem now is how to deal with the minorities.'

It was difficult not to let my almost open-mouthed astonishment betray itself. I fell silent.

For a while, Mr Goonetileke was silent too. He revived himself. 'Let me give you some advice. Your time would be best spent in looking at what is positive in Sri Lanka. These marginal topics will get you nowhere.'

I was silent.

Mr Goonetileke talked on. The island – as the statistics would confirm – had one of the lowest per capita incomes in the world. And yet, the literacy rate was high; life expectancy approached to developed country standards; infant mortality was extremely low. 'How do you explain these non-LDC (Less Developed Country) characteristics?'

I remained silent.

He confirmed his point with the appropriate statistics. These miracles had come about because of the notions of self-sacrifice inculcated by Buddhist doctrine. 'Our elite defied the Marxist model and analysis. Here the elite took the lead in securing the well-being of the masses. In what other country has that happened?'

No doubt it was out of such positive facts as those that he wove the chimerical constructions he paraded on the international conference circuit. How was it possible for him to take himself seriously? Did the principle of self-interest necessarily have to be so blind in its operations? Did it necessarily have to coexist with delusion and deception? Did the quest for 'identity', for 'roots', necessarily have to doom its disciples to untruth? The telephone shrilled. I rose, preparing for departure. He put the receiver down; he announced that someone else was waiting to see him.

'You must learn,' he repeated as he escorted me to the door, 'to look at what is positive.' He gave me a benevolent pat on the shoulder.

I promised I would try. 'The only difficulty,' I said, 'is that blood is such a bright red. It stands out. It has a way of forcing itself on the attention.'

His amiability persisted as he shut the door.

So ended my first encounter with the mental and spiritual make-up of the modern Sri Lankan intellectual.

*

The majority (i.e. the Sinhalese) may have achieved all their desires. Yet, to read the newspapers was to believe the island was in a condition approaching civil war.

'The President of the Gandhian Movement ... was taken into custody on Friday as the Government launched an intensified investigation into the activities of this group. The police found in his possession literature on guerrilla tactics ... a quantity of pornographical literature was also found ... Survey teams from the Land Commissioner's Department and Census and Statistics Department which rushed to Trincomalee on a Presidential directive have indicated that there is large-scale encroachment in the district ... According to their findings, most of the encroachers settled here by the Gandhian Movement are Indian labour from the [tea] estates ... Farms and extensive settlements had also taken place in the encroached area ... The investigation has revealed that one feature of the settlements was that they were situated on the borders of the area demarcated for the state of Eelam [the name conferred on the would-be independent state advocated by the Tamil separatists], whilst the areas between them and the Tamil-speaking areas were unoccupied. The purpose behind the creation of a buffer zone made up of displaced Indian labour appeared with the intent of presenting the Government with a fait accompli ... The colonisation programme had been given impetus following the communal disturbance in 1977 ... Under the cover of rehabilitation, the Tamils outside the proposed areas of Eelam were given financial inducement to settle in the area. Data has also been gathered on moves by certain individuals to harass and intimidate individuals from other communities in order to force them to leave the area. Evidence has also been unearthed of attempts to systematically eradicate signs of the culture of other communities.'

'... Considering the volatile situations prevailing, it is now time to act firmly to defuse the situation, before Sri Lanka becomes another Ireland. There is the school of thought which believes there is only one means of defeating an uprising – that is through extermination. They believe that the only way to control a territory that harbours resistance is to turn it into a desert. However, this theory is impractical in the fact that where these ends cannot be achieved the war is lost.'

*

They tell it more or less like this to the children.

A long, long time ago, when Gautama the future Buddha still walked the earth in human form, there lived in the region of Bengal a king and queen. To the royal couple, a beautiful daughter was born. Her beauty was beyond description and yet the omens were bad. For the astrologers attached to the court foretold evil things concerning the fate of this loveliest of princesses. They predicted that, unless strictly guarded, she would lead a life 'wild' and 'unbecoming'. The King and Queen, greatly alarmed by these tidings, did all that was humanly and royally possible to shelter the princess and so avert the fulfilment of the terrible prophecy. But destiny was not to be cheated by their wiles.

One day, eluding her attendants, she escaped from the confines of the palace and sought refuge with a caravan of merchants then encamped in the city. With them, she travelled westward as far as the region we call Gujerat. There, in the jungle, calamity befell the merchants. A gang of bandits attacked the caravan. Their leader was a fearsome fellow, the most ruthless of plunderers. His name was Sinha – which means 'lion'. Bewitched by the beauty of the runaway princess, he made her his captive and took her off with him to a cave deep in the jungle. There they lived many years. In time, the princess bore her bandit lover two children, a boy and a girl, Sinhabahu and Sinhasivali.

But, as the years passed, the princess found herself wearying of her wild and unbecoming life in a cave in the middle of the jungle. She yearned for the pleasures of the court life she had so wilfully abandoned; and so it came to pass that, for the second time, the princess ran away. Taking her son and daughter with her, she fled back to the country of her birth. Sinha was distraught with grief. Frenziedly, he searched for her, terrorising the countryside. The King, moved by the distress of the villagers, offered a generous reward to anyone who would bring him the head of the love-demented bandit. Against his mother's wishes, Sinhabahu volunteered to perform the dreadful task. He returned to the jungle in which he had passed his childhood. Sinha, on recognising him, ran forward with cries of joy. As he ran, arms outstretched to his son, Sinhabahu took aim and slew his father with an arrow. Triumphantly, he carried the head back to the court. During his absence, the king had died. Who more worthy to assume the vacant throne than the parricide? But Sinhabahu, suddenly overcome by remorse, relinquished the honour and exiled himself to the wilderness once roamed over by his bandit father. He cleared the land, founded villages and built a city, Sinhapura – the city of Sinha. He became king of this land, ruling 'wisely and justly'; and, for queen, he took his sister, Sinhasivali. Vijaya, his first-born, he proclaimed his heir.

But Vijaya was cursed with the temptation to wantonness that haunted his family. Like his grandfather, he took to a life of pillage and extortion. He and the seven hundred out-laws with which tradition credits him unleashed a reign of terror on the local populace, 'torturing and slaying not only cattle but sometimes even little innocent children' – until, finally, his father lost patience. Vijaya and his companions were interned and, to emphasise their disrepute, suffered the indignity of having one side of their heads shaved bare. Thus branded, they were put on board a not too seaworthy ship and consigned to the whims of the ocean.

It is told that the renegades made their landfall on the island of Lanka on the same day that Gautama died and so was finally released from the travail of rebirth and earthly existence. The island at that time was inhabited by aboriginal peoples, probably of Dravidian stock, worshippers of snakes and demons. With the arrival of Vijaya and his seven hundred companions, the ancient confrontation between 'Aryan' and Dravidian, the Light and the Dark, had found itself a new battle-ground, a new front line. As the invaders rested disconsolately on the seashore, a dog appeared. The animal approached Vijaya where he lay, sniffed at him and then scampered away into the bush. One of his companions set off in pursuit. When he failed to come back, Vijaya went off to search for him. Soon he came to a tank on the outskirts of a settlement. There he caught sight of the beautiful Kuveni, daughter of one of the aboriginal chieftains, sitting in the shade of a banyan tree, spinning thread. Vijaya, sword in hand, went up to her. It was to be a fateful encounter.

'Lady, hast thou not seen one of my men hereabouts?'

'Prince,' she replied, 'let be thy man awhile. First drink thou and bathe.'

Startled by her knowledge of his rank, Vijaya was seized with the superstitious fear that she might be of some demonic breed.

'Slave!' cried the Aryan warrior, 'give me back my man or I slay thee.' He grabbed her dark tresses.

She implored him to spare her life. 'I will give thee a kingdom and do thee a woman's service and other service as thou wilt.'

Her all too mortal terror calmed his fear. 'He had no doubt that she was as much a human being as he, though it might be of another race.'

She was of another race, but she was beautiful and she was the daughter of a powerful chieftain: Vijaya would make her his Queen. He vowed eternal devotion. 'The seed sown in this beautiful Lanka must be washed away,' he declared to her, 'the fields turned to waste-land and marsh, food-stuffs, fruit-seeds ... become unfit to eat, ere I prove unfaithful.'

Ceremoniously, 'with true Aryan courtesy' that greatly charmed Kuveni, he offered up to her the rice and other dishes prepared for the marriage feast. The good fortune that had taken him from the desolation of the seashore to Kuveni remained with him. For it so happened that in a neighbouring town there was gathered a large assembly of the aboriginal people come together to celebrate another marriage – that of the daughter of their King. On his wedding night Vijaya was roused from sleep by the noise of their revelry. He asked his bride its cause and, as Kuveni explained, an idea came to her. 'Destroy them all today,' she urged, 'this very night, my lord, for afterwards it will no longer be possible.' As the aboriginals danced and feasted, Vijaya and his seven hundred Aryan warriors fell upon the kinsfolk of the traitorous Kuveni. This massacre signalled the birth of the Sinhalese nation, the ascendancy of the Light over the Dark. The vanquished aboriginals retreated from their conquerors, taking refuge among the hills and jungles in the interior of the island.

The nascent Sinhalese nation spread out, founding towns and settlements, consolidating their rule. Kuveni, in the meanwhile, bore her husband two children. His courtiers petitioned Vijaya, urging that he have himself formally proclaimed and anointed their King. The idea appealed to him. But there was a problem. That problem was Kuveni. To him it was unimaginable that his future Queen, the consecrated mother of the Sinhalese, should be anything other than a 'Princess of his own Aryan race'. He might – as his chronicler says – have had a father's natural feeling for his offspring; but even so he recoiled from them, they being 'unlike him in colour' and therefore wholly unacceptable. Kingship, legitimacy, could not be nourished on such a racially compromised foundation. The impurity of his children made them seem like 'aliens' to him and 'his pride of race revolted at any but a pure Aryan succeeding to the Government which he had striven so laboriously to found.' His courtiers agreed: Kuveni, having exhausted her usefulness, had to be discarded.

An embassy, bearing a letter from Vijaya and many costly presents, was dispatched to the court of Madhura on the Indian mainland. The Madhurans responded enthusiastically to Vijaya's pleas for racial succour. More than a hundred Aryan maidens, all of the most faultless ancestry, volunteered to make the pilgrimage to Lanka. Chief among them was the King's own daughter. Nor was that the sum of their generosity. A profusion of craftsmen and artisans succumbed to the blandishments of the conquerors of Lanka. Among them were ' . . . carpenters, goldsmiths, weavers, garland makers, potters, tailors, leather workers, barbers, painters, basket-makers, turners, blacksmiths, washermen, conduit makers, lutenists, arrow-makers . . .'

Vijaya, hearing of the mission's success, summoned Kuveni. He revealed to her – Lanka's Caliban – his change of heart and his change of plan. 'When shipwrecked and forlorn,' she said to him, 'I found thee and thy men food and home . . . Didst thou not then know that I was of the Yakkha race? . . . I bore thee children, husband mine. Canst thou now leave me and love another?' Vijaya was, perhaps, touched by her predicament. He offered her gold and assured her she might live unmolested wheresoever she might choose within his kingdom. Kuveni spurned his gold. As for living unmolested wheresoever she might choose – what was that to her? To her the soft light of the moon was like ' . . . the blaze of a red-hot iron ball, the cool, spice-laden breezes of the sandal groves, hot and unwelcome . . . Alas! Alas! How can I soothe my heart?' Taking her two children, she left behind her the Aryan-dominated lands, wandering away towards the hills and jungles, making her way back to those whom she had betrayed. When they saw her coming, her kinsfolk rushed upon her. Death was swift. Vijaya made a queen out of his Madhura princess; the maidens who had accompanied her were distributed among his nobles. Lanka had been made safe for the Aryans.

*

The artist, waving me over to his presence, invited me to sit beside him.

'Tonight,' he announced, cigarette smoke coiling from his nostrils, 'you find me in a celebratory mood. Later, I shall take you to my club and we shall drink arrack.'

I looked around the hall. Apart from a loitering bell-boy and ourselves, there was no one else present, no discernible cause for his rapture. Did this capricious outburst of good humour have any connection, I wondered, with the strange little scene I had witnessed the previous evening? Not long after darkness had fallen, with the lights of the food-stalls flaring out festally on the Green, I had been startled to see a European woman, in full bridal regalia and carrying a bouquet of anthurium lilies, come running in out of the night into the hall. In her wake followed her somewhat bemused, dark-suited groom, his jacket adorned with a spray of small white carnations. She had led him up to one of the paintings. Together they had stood before the canvas, she speaking agitatedly in a breathless undertone, flourishing her bouquet, he nodding a trifle sullenly, looking alternately at her and at the painting; and frowning with inarticulate perplexity at both. Leaving him, she had clattered across the room, her gold-coloured shoes flashing as she lifted her billowing gown, to the artist who had risen from his chair. She embraced him, raining a flurry of kisses on his cheeks, speaking into his ear in that same breathless undertone. She was, I saw, crying a little, soaking up her tears with a lacy handkerchief. Still crying, her dark-suited groom in pursuit, she had run, like some demented Cinderella, back out into the night from which she had come.

The artist, wiggling his sandalled feet, lowered his voice. 'Things seem to be looking up for me at last,' he said. 'Earlier today I had a visit from my friend the Italian ambassador.' He paused, widening his eyes at me. Lowering his voice even further and angling his head towards me in a confiding manner, he went on. 'There is a very good chance I might be travelling to Europe quite soon.'

I tried to convey pleasure and surprise at the disclosure.

He permitted himself a smothered, throaty half-laugh. 'I may be going to Rome – Roma as they say over there.' Ridding himself of his cigarette, he began to crack his knuckles. 'Yes, my friend, I may be going to Roma quite soon. They would like some of my paintings for an exhibition they are having. Their recognition is very heartening for me.'

I tendered my congratulations.

'That is why – tonight, this very night – you and I shall be drinking arrack.' He coughed, he slapped his chest, he jiggled his sandalled feet. His restlessness, the glitter of his gaze, made me suspect that he had already been at the arrack. He placed a cautionary finger on my wrist. 'You must promise not to tell anyone. Here in Sri Lanka there are many jealous people. If they were to hear of my good fortune, who knows what they might be tempted to do? Talent such as mine always makes enemies.' He lit another cigarette. 'I must say nothing until my friend the ambassador makes the official announcement.'

I vowed that, until then, my lips would remain sealed.

He was too agitated to sit still. He rose and paced about, glancing at the paintings lining the walls. Eventually, he came back to me, perching himself on the arm of my chair. 'The exhibition in Roma is to be about Peace. That is the theme. That is why my presence is necessary. Peace On Earth . . . Peace Among Men . . . I cannot remember which exactly.'

'They mean much the same thing,' I said.

He stared at me as though their synonymity had not previously occurred to him; as if I had enunciated a revelation of truly arresting profundity.

'That is so,' he murmured. 'Peace On Earth, Peace Among Men – they are the same thing when you stop and think about it.' He bestowed on me an admiring shake of his handsome, greying head. 'That is what my paintings are about, you realise. Peace – on Earth, among Men, in Heaven. Everywhere. I make no distinction. My friend the ambassador understood that straightaway. He would like me to take my message of peace to his countrymen. He tells me that in Italia they are much interested in such things.' He started to pace again. Coming back from his wanderings, he perched himself once more on the arm of my chair. Again he placed a cautionary finger on my wrist. 'But we must wait for the official announcement from the Embassy. His Excellency would be annoyed if I let the cat out of the bag. When he makes the announcement, then we shall see.' He produced one of his strangulated laughs. 'Watch how they shall come crowding about me, all these people who call themselves Sri Lankans.' His truculent stare roamed the empty room, lingered on the loitering bell-boy. 'I shall be dignified. I will not boast. Nor will I shower recriminations on their heads. That is not in my nature.' He smiled altruistically. 'I shall accept their congratulations as now I accept their neglect. I will not gloat.'

'When is the official announcement likely to be made?'

Ah . . . about that he was not entirely sure. Not even his friend the ambassador was entirely sure. It could happen in a few days – or it could take a few weeks. There were still one or two minor details to be tidied up by the ambassador's friends in Roma.

I could not resist enquiring about the scene I had witnessed the previous evening.

'So! You saw it! You saw it with your very own eyes!' He was obviously delighted. 'You saw with your own eyes how Karen came straight to me from the church. Such is the power of art, my friend.' Karen was Danish and, for the last couple of years, had been resident in Colombo, attached to one or another of the international aid agencies. During that time, she had become one of his most steadfast devotees, captivated by the spirituality evident in his every brush-stroke. 'It is the living proof of what I have said to you before. Only the foreigners appreciate me. Only they see my genius.' He jumped up from the arm of the chair. 'Come. I will show you.' He led me to the painting before which Karen had stood with her bewildered groom. 'Have a good look,' he commanded. 'Maybe you too will see what touched the heart of that beautiful woman.'

I scrutinised with care the blurred, amorphous shapes mooning across the muddied depths of the canvas, willing myself to be touched by the magic that had so moved the heart of a beautiful woman. Behind me I could hear the artist's deep, intent breathing.

'Do you see?' he asked impatiently. 'Do you see?'

Was it possible that he himself did not?

'The painting certainly has a very peaceful quality . . .'

'So you too can see!' He sounded relieved. 'Do you know what my dear Karen said when she first saw me working on this painting in my studio? She said, "You are painting my life! This is my life taking shape under your hands on that piece of canvas!" That is what she said to me. And that is what she was trying to say to her husband last night. "If you cannot understand this painting," she said to him, "You cannot understand the woman you have just married, you will never understand my life." ' He backed away from me, hands thrust into his trouser-pockets. 'I'm afraid, though, he did not seem to fully understand.' He swayed his handsome head, mockingly sad.

I examined the picture afresh, searching its muddy depths for the clues that had so far eluded me. Enlightenment did not descend. That it could represent Karen's – or anyone else's – life was as bewildering to me as it must have been to her husband so precipitately dragged away from the solemnities of his wedding ritual.

Karen, naturally enough, had wanted to buy the painting that mirrored her life. But Karen did not have the money to do so. I was a little taken aback by this: the employees of international aid agencies are not normally poor. Generally, they conduct their self-sacrificial life quite stylishly.

'I said she could pay me in instalments,' the artist said. 'But that she would not do.' He shrugged.

And how indeed, I reflected, could one buy the mirror of one's life on the instalment plan?

'Is it,' I ventured, 'very expensive?'

The artist was both nonchalant and evasive. 'The financial reward is, of course, secondary to me. I do not believe the value of art can truly be expressed in material terms. But, at the same time, even artists have to live.'

I gathered from this that his asking price was high, mirroring the going rate.

It was a bad night for transport, not a taxi or a scooter-rickshaw to be had in the vicinity of the hotel. The Green was emptied of its food-stalls and promenaders. Here and there solitary figures skulked on the grass or slunk along the sea-front bathed in the glow of the blue lamps. The Green, at this comparatively late hour, was given over to its pimps, its 'masseurs', its drug merchants.

'In a just world,' the artist said, 'we would not have to roam the streets like this. In a just world I would have been able to drive you to my club in my own car.' He sighed a long-suffering sigh. 'However, not to worry. We will find some means of getting there in the end.'

I was gripped by a momentary alarm: someone was tugging at my shirt-sleeve. 'Sir ... sir ...' Crouched at my feet, a cupped palm outstretched, was a shrivelled tangle of flesh and bone. 'Sir ... sir ...' I looked to the artist for support, for guidance. He, however, seemed altogether unaware of the creature and its grappling fingers.

'An artist must accustom himself to martyrdom,' he continued, ignoring my futile struggle to free myself. 'We may hope for reward but we must not expect it. The wise man hopes but does not expect. Struggle ... struggle ... that is all.' Lifting his head, he stared out towards the foam-flecked glimmer of the indifferent ocean. Hands in pockets, he jingled his small change, inflaming the passions of the limpet-like creature clinging to me, digging its fingers into my flesh.

'Sirs ... sirs ... I can be of help to you ...'

'The artist must rest his hope in the generations to come. He must fix his attention on those distant horizons ...' He jingled his coins.

Despairingly, I dropped a couple of rupees into the outstretched palm. Instantly, my arm was released, the creature vanishing.

'You should not have given anything.' The artist frowned.

'I was told that beggary is no shame in Sri Lanka, that the giving of alms is a virtue.' I rubbed my smarting flesh.

'That is true. The giving of alms is a virtue. But we don't give alms to scoundrels. There is no merit in that kind of giving.'

Out of nowhere a scooter-rickshaw appeared, easing to a halt beside us.

'Sirs ... sirs ...' The cripple's face loomed out from

under the scooter's canopy. It grinned at us. 'Here you are, sirs. All yours.' Suddenly agile, suddenly no longer a cripple, he jumped out of the scooter, saluting us.

The artist maintained his imperturbability. 'Climb in, my friend. I told you we would find something sooner or later.'

Our unacknowledged benefactor skipped away into the darkness.

'To the Seals.' The artist's tone was peremptory.

'Where Seals?' Our ragged chauffeur was sleepy and sullen.

The artist was dumbfounded by the man's ignorance. 'This is unheard of. Utterly astonishing. What is this Sri Lanka of ours coming to?' He spoke in Sinhalese to the driver.

We set off at last, rattling and vibrating through the cool night. The artist, settling himself, lit a cigarette. 'Utterly amazing.' He exhaled a cloud of incredulous smoke. 'These peasants seem to be getting everywhere. Such a thing has never before happened to me.'

'Tell me about the Seals,' I said.

It was a most exclusive place. Top-notch. Very long waiting-list for membership . . . very expensive . . . established by the British in colonial days . . . 'In those days, the natives could not become members. Now, of course, that is all changed.' All the same, the waiting-list was long. Very long.

'The Seals,' I hazarded, 'is a funny name.'

He laughed. 'That is because it is mainly for the swimming. Seals are great swimmers, is that not so? You will see when you get there.'

When we were about a quarter of a mile or so from our destination, the driver was ordered to stop. 'From here,' the artist said, 'we walk.'

I betrayed signs of puzzlement as I climbed out; he showed all the symptoms of embarrassment.

'To be seen,' the artist said, 'to arrive at the Seals in a scooter is . . . how would you say?'

'Non-U?'

He did not understand.

'Not top-notch.'

'Ah . . . yes, yes . . .' Of course, as an artist, he himself was not a subscriber to such prejudices. He was far, far above such things. To prove the point, he indicated his sandalled feet. 'You must have observed by now that I am something of a bohemian.'

'Quite.'

'But very few are like me.' He reassumed his mantle of martyrdom. 'In Sri Lanka the bohemians are not many.'

'Quite.'

'At the Seals,' he clarified in an outburst of candour, 'they do not care for these scooters.'

'Are they banned from the premises?'

'I would not say "banned". But the Seals do not like them. The management committee feels that . . .' He groped for words.

'Don't they object to people coming in on foot?'

He smiled. 'For an artist like myself they make allowances.'

It being my turn to say 'ah', I obliged.

In the soft, jasmine-scented evening we sat out in the garden, within splashing distance of the swimming-pool. To our table was borne a bottle of arrack, a bucket of ice, glasses. The brown bodies of joyful Seals thrashed and glistened under the floodlights. We drank with abandon.

'May I look at your hand, my friend?'

I surrendered it to him. 'It is not that I am an expert in palmistry,' he said, 'nor is it that I am a believer in the occult.' He sipped his arrack. The Seals thrashed the water; the Seals glistened.

He traced the wavering trajectory of my 'head-line'.

'Like me,' he declared, 'You too one day will be world-famous.'

I looked demure.

'You have,' he added, 'the temperament of an artist. Like me, you suffer, you have many tribulations to bear. Such is the fate of all artists.' He released my hand. 'Mind you,' he muttered, sipping his arrack, 'you must not believe such nonsense. It is all fraud, all charlatanism. I myself am curious but I do not believe. It is meaningless.' He gestured vehemently – and, in so doing, swept the bucket of ice off the table. It clattered on to the flagstones. Startled Seals gazed at us with consternation. We both pretended not to notice.

So, I was not destined for world fame after all; I couldn't lay claim to an artistic temperament. Arrack is a saddening drink, conducive to fatalism. Lugubriously I considered my relinquished palm.

'It is all fraud, all charlatanism.' The artist, gloomy now, surveyed the starry heavens, but seemed to find no consolation there. 'Of that I have cast-iron proof.'

An attendant came running over to our table. With discretion, he retrieved the ice-bucket. 'More ice, sir?'

'Ice ... what is ice? It is a question I have often asked myself.' Bending down, the artist picked up from the flagstones the melting remains of one of the cubes. He contemplated it with intensity. 'It is all a terrible mystery. Like life itself.' He watched as the cube melted away. 'A moment ago it was ice, now it is water. In my art I try to explore such mysteries. My friend, the Italian ambassador, recognises that. Life is like an ice-cube. We too melt as we grow old.' He wagged his handsome head as he dried his hands with a paper napkin.

The attendant rattled the bucket. 'More ice, sir?'

The artist waved him away. 'Cast-iron proof ...' He poured more arrack into our glasses. 'I have been to many, many of those charlatans. I cannot tell you how much money I have wasted. Utterly worthless.' He leaned forward, bringing his face close to mine. 'Would you believe that not one – not one! – recognised that I was an artist?'

I proffered my incredulity.

'It is true. That is how I know they are all frauds and charlatans. They would say I was big businessman. They would say I was doctor, engineer, lawyer. They would say I am this and I am that and I am the other. Not one recognised that I was an artist.' He slammed his fist down on the metal table. Just in time I caught the toppling arrack bottle. Seals stared in renewed consternation.

The artist surveyed the sky. Still he seemed to find no consolation there.

'Let me ask you this question.' He exhaled clouds of smoke. 'What is culture?'

'That too is one of the terrible mysteries,' I said. 'At least as mysterious as the nature of ice.'

He levelled his index finger at me. 'I will tell you what culture is in this Sri Lanka of ours. At any rate, I will tell you what the Ministry of Culture believes it is.' So far as they were concerned it meant, above all else, the taking abroad of troupes of dancers. 'Can you guess why they are so crazy about this dancing?'

I looked nonplussed.

'Because it requires many officials to supervise. That is why.' While the dancers were lodged in three-star hotels (or worse), the officials lavished on themselves five-star treatment in the Babylons of the Western world. 'That is what culture means in this Sri Lanka of ours.' Himself – he was not even considered. 'To them, a great artist like me is nothing. Hailed in Roma, neglected in Colombo.' He was beginning to tremble with outrage. At one point the Ministry of Culture had promised to stage an exhibition of his work. Nothing had ever been done about it. On the other hand, the childish daubs of an eight-year-old relative of the President had received widespread acclaim. The 'opening' had been a glittering social occasion. In the end it was only through the intervention of his friend, the Italian ambassador, that he had been able to stage the current exhibition – to which no one came. Why was he so ignored and despised? He was ignored and despised because he refused to cheapen his artistic vision; because he licked no one's boots; because he refused to become 'commercial'. 'You will see nothing of Sri Lanka in my work,' he said.

'Why is that?'

'Because I am a universalist. A citizen of the world.' He drank with defiant gusto; with reddening eyes; drying his cracked lips on his shirt-sleeves. It was a topsy-turvy world that allowed a labourer on a building-site to earn more than he did. He was outdone by the migrants who sold their elementary skills to the sheikdoms of the Persian Gulf, who, bartering their pride for financial reward, came back and built themselves fine houses of brick, who bought themselves mini-buses – a mode of transport he was forced to use because he had no car of his own and could not always afford taxis. Some of these tycoons owned two . . . three . . . mini-buses. If it were not for the encouragement and support of his friend the Italian ambassador, the fanatical devotion of Karen, he would probably have killed himself long before now. He pounded the table with a clenched fist. This time my reflexes failed me; the bottle of arrack tottered, fell and, rolling out of reach, shattered on the flagstones. Fortunately, it was almost empty. 'Perhaps it is time to go.' The artist hauled himself unsteadily to his feet, oblivious of the attendant who had come hurrying up with dust-pan and brush; oblivious, too, of the disapprobation of the Seals assembled round the pool. I wanted to believe that he would be saved from humiliation by his reputation for bohemianism.

And, to a degree, fate was kind to the artist. As we stood at the gates of the Club searching for a taxi, a Mercedes Benz slithered to a shiny halt. A woman's voice called the artist by name. 'I expect,' he whispered as we hastened forward, 'these are admirers of mine.'

So, indeed, the couple seemed to be. The artist was greeted with respect. Courteously, he was ushered into the back seat, the woman placing herself beside him. I was ushered into the front.

'We have been meaning to come to your exhibition,' the woman said. 'I hope it is going well.'

'Given the circumstances, I cannot complain.' The artist, hands on knees, was prim.

'How long will it run?'

'Of that I am not certain. I may be going abroad quite soon. Some people in Rome are clamouring for me to go there. My friend, the Italian ambassador, is making the arrangements.'

'That is nice,' the woman said.

'Do you know the ambassador?' the artist asked.

'We have met him,' the husband said. 'We know most of those Embassy types.'

'The ambassador is a very good friend of mine,' the artist said. 'A personal friend, you know. He is what I would call a human being.'

'Yes,' the woman remarked reflectively. 'The ambassador is a human being.'

'In Sri Lanka today,' the artist said, 'it is not easy to find human beings.'

'I agree with you,' the woman rejoined after another suitably reflective interlude. 'Human beings – real human beings – are in very short supply nowadays.'

In a spirit of amity we sped through the Colombo night.

*

He was a Tamil and a Christian. We do not, however, know his name. All we have is his personal testimony. 'I have only related incidents which I have personally seen or heard,' he wrote . . . 'I swear by the Holy Bible that everything written in this diary is true.' The events described occurred in the month of July, in the year 1983. Human beings – real human beings – were in especially short supply during that time.

He had set off for work as usual from his house in the Colombo suburb of Maharagama. As he approached the main road, he noticed the first signs of trouble. A row of small shops was on fire. A turbulent crowd was roaming the roadway. He asked an onlooker what was the cause of the disturbance.

'They have killed thirteen of our people in Jaffna,' the man replied. 'We must avenge their deaths. We must kill all the Tamils. That is what we are doing.'

The man was referring to an ambush that had taken place the previous day in the northern, Tamil-dominated region of the island. Thirteen Sinhalese soldiers had been killed by separatist guerrillas.

Still curiously determined to get to his place of work, he went on to the bus-stop. The bus when it came was crowded and its progress was slow. Marauding bands armed with clubs and knives, axes and iron bars, roamed the roads. All along the route he saw shops in flames and heard the screams of those being butchered. The mob was stopping cars and mini-buses, dragging out their occupants for interrogation, demanding that all Tamils declare themselves.

He watched cars being smashed and set on fire.

He watched a man, axe in hand, hack to limbless death a young boy.

Out of the fire and the smoke rose cries of terror.

A van exploded into flames. It was only when he heard the screams coming from within that he realised there were people penned inside; that those within were being roasted alive.

A group of men pushed their way into the bus. They ordered the driver to choose them a Tamil. He picked out one of the women passengers. As the men bore down on her, she tried to erase from her forehead the *kumkum* – the red disc of powder, the emblem of her Tamilhood now become her death sentence.

He watched as her belly was ripped open with a broken bottle. In the ensuing stampede, he escaped in the melee of passengers, melting away into the crowd.

The mutilated woman was manhandled by her executioners through a window of the bus. She was covered with blood. She was screaming. Petrol was poured over her and she was set ablaze.

The spectators clapped and danced.

As her body burned, a procession of Buddhist monks appeared. Arms flailing, voices raised in a delirium of exhortation, they summoned the Sinhalese to put all Tamils to death.

He managed to survive unscathed the four-mile journey back to his house. For, though Sinhalese folk-wisdom would have you believe otherwise, it is not always possible in Sri Lanka to distinguish at a glance between those whom you must hate and those whom you must cherish. ('I find it difficult to persuade myself,' a Sinhalese essayist wrote some twenty years ago in the wake of another outbreak of communal carnage, 'to believe that the two major communities of Ceylon are influenced by racial and religious prejudices. Racially we are closer to the Dravidians than some South Indian communities who, though Dravidians by language, claim, rightly or wrongly, ninety percent Aryan blood.') Colombo's murderers, looters and incendiarists often had to rely on the information derived from the electoral registers to assist them in the task of enemy identification. Their blood-lust was, in effect, regulated by the bureaucratic endeavours of the Civil Service. Before the axes could be wielded, before the petrol bombs could be thrown, before the pillaging could begin, a little paperwork was necessary.

Hope stirred when he caught sight of an army patrol. But he shrank back when he discovered that the soldiers were doing nothing to discourage the mayhem. In his district an unnatural quiet still prevailed. On that day he was alone. The family was away in Jaffna – where they had gone to attend the wedding of a relative. He took what precautions he could. He dug three trenches in the garden. In these he interred the family's valuables.

Towards noon, he became aware of the first sounds of commotion on the street. Buses and jeeps had arrived. Out of these came men brandishing knives and swords. Some carried those indispensable electoral lists. It was fortunate that he had neglected to register himself.

He watched as windows were broken in three houses selected for attack on the opposite side of the street. He watched as petrol bombs were tossed inside. He heard the screams of the occupants as the fires took hold. Retreating from the window, he lit a candle to St. Anthony, invoking his protection. He tried to pray but his concentration was disturbed by the screaming of the men and women and children who were burning to death not many yards away. He returned to the window.

Two girls were being dragged along the street. He knew them – they were sisters. One, still a child, was about eleven years old, the other about eighteen. The captors were arguing over the fate of their captives. Eventually, one of the men seized the younger of the girls. With his knife, he scythed away her hair. There was laughter when the elder girl fell on her knees before them.

He was watching from his window when another man, carrying an axe, stepped forward.

Seizing the child – she whose hair had been scythed – he chopped off her head.

The older girl – she who had fallen on her knees – was stripped naked.

When there were no more volunteers, when there was nothing left worth the violating, petrol was poured over the two bodies. They were set alight.

Later that evening, with Colombo festive under smoky skies, he was taken, under irresolute police protection, to join the thousands who had been dumped in the refugee camp set up at the airport.

*

When I first saw him he was carrying a tattered Penguin edition of the plays of Aristophanes. Tall – well over six-foot – and stoop-shouldered, he was so exiguously stretched out that, when seen in profile, he gave the impression of being one-dimensional. He was dark for a Sinhalese, so dark as to call into question his Aryanism. His name was Tissa – 'friend of the gods': a title much associated with the ancient kings of Lanka. Tissa was a friend of sorts of the artist. Hearing from him that I was a writer, he had come to introduce himself. I took to Tissa straightaway, moved by his frailty, by his painful candour, by his hopeless gentleness.

'He's a simple fellow,' the artist said, 'but you might find him amusing. You must not expect too much. Remember he's a country person,' he proceeded with casual disparagement, 'and ignorant. Tissa says one day he will kill himself and I believe him. I do what little I can for him in the meantime.'

I stared at Tissa – he was standing at a discreet distance from us, waiting to be called – smiling with patient expectation behind his gold-rimmed spectacles. He was so thinly stretched out that he seemed to have difficulty holding himself upright. His torso was drooping, wilting, into concavity as he stood there, clutching his Aristophanes. When we were introduced he drooped so far forward I feared he might not be able to straighten up again without doing himself some mischief.

'I too am something of a writer,' he revealed without affection, without any hint of presumption in his manner as, with an awkward twist and a turn, he elevated himself into a semblance of perpendicularity. 'It is why I wanted to meet you.' His eyes narrowed into a reticent smile behind those gold-rimmed spectacles. The bony rods of his fingers caressed the dog-eared edges of the Aristophanes. Trousers and shirt hung loosely on his spare, skeletal frame. He had written several novels and dozens of short stories. 'But my writings are all in my own language, all in Sinhalese. That is why I did not bring anything of mine to show you.' His English was delivered with effort but, at the same time, it possessed a queer and alluring precision, each word falling like a polished stone from his narrow lips. Some of his work had been published locally. 'But only in the paperback,' he clarified with a self-deprecating flick of a stick-like wrist. 'It is cheaper that way.' He lowered himself into a chair. 'Mainly, however, I write for the pleasure of it. It is not possible to earn a living from the literary life in Sri Lanka.' He was ill at ease on the chair, arranging and rearranging his arms and legs, discovering no suitable resting places for those cumbersome extensions of himself.

'Tissa works in the Survey Department,' the artist put in. 'What he does there nobody has ever been able to find out.

He knows nothing of map-making, nothing of trigonometry. Ask him.'

'It is true,' Tissa agreed readily enough. 'I know nothing of the making of maps. My job is a . . . I cannot pronounce the word though I can spell it. My job is a s-i-n-e-c-u-r-e.'

I supplied the pronunciation.

'For that I am grateful to you,' Tissa said. 'Yes – you may say I have a sinecure. The Survey Department pays me thirteen hundred rupees a month for doing nothing at all.' His lenses reflected the revolving ceiling fans.

'Which he squanders on books and on arrack,' the artist said. 'Is that not so, Tissa? You neglect your wife, you neglect your four children.' The artist turned to me. 'He lacks utterly a sense of responsibility.'

'That is so,' Tissa confirmed, simultaneously earnest and unabashed. 'I do not have much of a sense of responsibility. I love to drink arrack and I love to buy books.' He placed a pair of vein-ridged hands on his knees, tangling together the ribs of his bony fingers. 'My vices are books and the booze. It cannot be helped.' He untangled his fingers, swung his knees apart. 'Not, however, sex. Sex I do not much care for. Booze and books – those are my vices!' A dreaminess dimmed his eyes. 'I have more than one thousand volumes in my library,' he said. He embarked on a listing of the authors whose works burdened his shelves. As he recited the litany of famous names, the upper reaches of him drooped into concavity, he swung his knees, angled his arms this way and that, meshed and unmeshed his fingers. 'What is more, I do not buy just to put on the shelf. I have read them all. Every single one.'

'He may have read these thousand books of his,' the artist intervened. 'But ask this of him – how much does he understand?'

'It is true,' Tissa conceded, 'that I do not understand everything I read. Three times I have read about Mr Finnegan's wake. Still I do not make of it head or tail.' A look of great sorrow passed over his face.

'Nor do I,' I said.

Tissa's face lit up. 'Is it so?' he asked. 'Is it really so? Who then really understands it?'

'One or two professors of English.'

Tissa removed his spectacles. He polished the lenses on the sleeve of his shirt. 'Then I do not feel so bad,' he said, holding his spectacles towards the light, squinting at the smears on the lenses. 'But why write a book nobody except professors of English can understand? It is supposed to be a great masterpiece, is it not?'

'The great masterpieces of art are never easily understood.' The artist's gaze travelled gravely round the walls of the empty hall. 'The great artist is always ahead of his time. I sympathise with this Mr Finnegan you are talking about.'

'I would like you to come to my house,' Tissa said. 'I would like to show you my library.' He readjusted his arms, his legs. 'I must warn you, though, that I live in humble circumstances. The facilities are elementary.' He stressed each syllable of this last word.

The artist was looking anxiously at me. 'It is a long way to Tissa's house,' he remarked. 'It takes two hours or more to get there.'

'It is too far for you?' Tissa blinked watchfully at me.

'No,' I answered, 'it isn't too far for me.'

The artist rose, shrugged and walked away from us.

Tissa said, 'He does not want for you to come. My invitation to you has displeased him. Why?'

'I do not know,' I said. It was indeed a curious little drama. The artist was standing in one of the doorways, his hands clasped behind his back, looking out across the hazy Green.

'It is because I am not one of the great ones,' Tissa said.

When Tissa had gone (he had a bus to catch), the artist called me over. 'You are going to Tissa's house?'

I nodded.

'That is most unwise of you.'

'Why?'

'I told you. Tissa is a simple fellow. A country person. What do you want with such an ignorant person? What can you gain from him?'

'The gain,' I said, remembering what he had said to me about 'material reward' on another occasion, 'is of secondary importance to me.'

If he detected my mockery, he chose to side-step it. 'Tomorrow I was planning to introduce you to my friend, the Italian ambassador.' He blew a perfect smoke ring. 'He has invited me over to his residence to have a drink with him. I was going to ask him if I could bring you along with me.'

I was silent.

Suddenly he changed tack. 'Did you notice, my friend, how that rich fellow – he's a millionaire, you know, a *very* big man – did you notice how he made his wife sit in the back of the car next to me?'

I must have let my perplexity show. Violently, he stubbed out his cigarette, a token of his intensifying annoyance. 'Don't you remember what happened that night I took you to my club? Don't you remember the big car that stopped for us?'

'I remember.'

'Putting his wife in the back was an honour to me. That was his way of showing his respect for me.' For the second time he turned his back on me.

I suspected that our friendship was on the rocks.

*

Tissa was appalled when I suggested we hire a car for our little excursion. 'Do you have so much money to waste?' he asked. Hire of a car, he explained, would cost the equivalent of a week's salary for him. Even though it was I who would be paying, I felt ashamed and abandoned the idea. 'We shall go by the mini-bus. We shall travel the way the people travel.' Taking me by the arm, he led me out into the blistering morning. 'When in Sri Lanka,' he said, 'you must do as the Sri Lankans do. That is always best.' He walked with energetic strides, his shadow darting out like a snake from the worn heels of his leather shoes. As before, he was carrying a book – but not, I noticed, the Aristophanes. Its place had been taken by the novel of a fashionable and best-selling American writer. One had to ask oneself what meaning such a work – shamelessly rooted in the narcissism engendered by Manhattan's psycho-analytical couches – could possibly have for someone like Tissa. It certainly had had none for me when I had tried to read it. Aristophanes represented a far more comprehensible choice.

'Are you enjoying that?' I indicated the book.

'Oh – one must enjoy. It is supposed to be a very great book. Look at all these things that have been said about it.' He showed me the lines of lavish praise reproduced on the back cover. 'The writer has been here. I went to the reading he gave at the Information Service of the United States.'

My heart sank at the sight of the crowd milling about the mini-bus halt. Colombo seemed to be emptying itself for the New Year festivities.

'Was the reading well-attended?'

'I myself could find only standing-room.'

Modish American writing, travelling on the wings of American money, power and prestige, penetrates everywhere. In the most improbable corners of the globe, where no one has ever caught sight of a psychoanalyst's couch, you will see its products – most as ephemeral as mayflies – being avidly consumed by those who pride themselves on their contemporaneity; whose hunger for literary up-to-dateness is indistinguishable from their hunger for patched and faded jeans. These parochial effusions mock the tired old ideal of universality. Once, when I happened to be living in New York, I began, as a recreation, to make a list of the books hailed each week as masterpieces. If I had accepted at face value all the claims made, I would have had to believe that, during that year alone, more works of staggering import had been published in that city than in all recorded human history.

It did not look possible, but Tissa somehow managed to shoulder himself and me on board the mini-bus. Even more miraculously, he was able to find space for us beside the driver – at the expense of a boy who was summarily dispatched by the latter to the densely populated nether regions

of the vehicle. 'Sit! Sit!' Tissa pushed me into the space
vacated by the boy. He manoeuvred himself on to the metallic
shield of the gear-box, contorting his legs and arms into
spidery angularity. A yellow-skinned man, his head swathed
in towelling, shared my seat. Eyes half-closed and glazed
with vacancy, he was moaning softly and trembling. A spasm
of coughing convulsed his frail body. When the bus jerked
and shuddered into motion, he collapsed against me in a
fiery, invertebrate heap. I indicated my alarm to Tissa, but
he seemed unperturbed, his response lost amid the clatter of
the engine. Opening his book, he started to read. I tried to
ignore the moaning and trembling of my companion, the
sudden spasms of coughing, the fieriness of the flesh huddled
against me.

We progressed slowly in the holiday traffic, Colombo
unwinding itself in a charmless sprawl. Clamorous crowds
flooded along the pavements, milling about the food-stalls
and liquor shops. I breathed in dust, the swirling fumes of
petrol and overheated oil. Tissa, detached, read his book
with unbroken concentration, wetting the tip of his index
finger as he turned the pages. It was not easy to discern at
what point Colombo ended and the countryside began. Only
at rare intervals did the narrow road cease to be fringed by
settlement, did the landscape open out to reveal a vista.
Gradually, though, the traffic lessened in intensity and the
light was softened by groves of coconut palms through which,
occasionally, one caught glimpses of the grey ocean or saw
the broad, dark-watered expanse of an inlet bordered by
mangrove. On the verandas of little bungalows with tiled
roofs older men and women stared at the monotonous parade
of pedestrians and slow-pedalling cyclists and bullock-drawn
carts. One felt, looking at the endless procession filing under
the ribbed patterns of light and shadow falling across the
narrow roadway, that they were coming from nowhere in
particular and going nowhere in particular: an elaborate
puppetry invisibly impelled into perpetual but meaningless
motion.

Spectrally, against the blueness of the sky, there floated

into view an enormous white dome. From the apex of the glacially pale hemisphere rose a tall, golden spire. Its hyperbolic bulk shimmered like an iceberg in the sunlight. Cars, buses, lorries, carts were halted along the roadsides, giving the place the look of a caravanserai. Nearby, its dark waters fringed by mangrove, was a broad inlet. We slowed to a stop. Our fellow passengers disembarked. The sick man, reviving somewhat, was helped to his feet by the driver. He too went out.

'What's happening? What's this place?'

'One of our modern temples.' Tissa looked up abstractedly from his book. 'Our rich men think they gain merit by giving the money to build such places.' He blinked towards its glaring whiteness. 'Everyone stops here. They say prayers, make offerings, ask for blessing. I myself do not believe in such superstitious practices.' He uncoiled himself, straightening his cumbersome arms and legs.

I watched my sick companion, coughing, tottering, make his way into the paved precincts of the temple.

'Would you like to see?' Tissa unfolded himself. 'We will, though, have to take off our shoes. It is most bothersome.'

We entered the spacious courtyard, we took off our shoes, we climbed the stairs leading to the inner sanctum. Under the phlegmatic gaze of the attendant monks, worshippers processed past the main altar adorned with brazen images and heaped with offerings of sweet-smelling flowers. An odour of incense thickened the warm air. On the walls were painted panels illustrating episodes from the Jataka, the cycle of tales describing the meritorious acts of the Buddha in his previous existences. These were rendered in a cheerful, comic-book style. We progressed, the floor warm under our bare feet, round the perimeter of the dome, inspecting the paintings. As we went along, Tissa supplied an ironical commentary on the events depicted. Returning to the sunlit courtyard, we reclaimed our shoes. Outside, cars, buses, lorries were arriving and departing; pilgrims squatted in the shade of the trees; the dark waters of the inlet wrinkled and rippled in the transient breezes.

'I am not at all a religious man.' Tissa, bending awkwardly, knotted the laces of his worn leather shoes. 'I believe in nothing.' He laughed as he drew himself erect. 'I do not even believe in Nirvana.' His ironic gaze rested on a group of smooth-skinned monks who, with stately gait, were ascending the stairs to the inner sanctum. He looked at me. 'Do I shock you?'

'No . . .'

With his shirt-sleeve, he dried the droplets of sweat on his forehead. 'You – what are you? What do you believe concerning the gods?'

What did I believe concerning the gods? The question was an arresting one. Religion had played little or no part in my life and I was a stranger to the kind of reverences and loyalties bred and expressed by it. True enough in my dim Trinidad past there had been those gatherings of the family to celebrate some of the more important festivals in the Hindu religious calendar. But their actual sacred significance had always been lost on me. No one had ever taken the trouble to explain; while I – and perhaps this is just as curious – had never taken the trouble to solicit an explanation. Religion, at best, was ritual – the sing-song drone of the pundits, the ringing of bells, the caterwauling of conch-horns, the suffocating odours of incense. Those who could have provided enlightenment were unapproachable and bad-tempered on such occasions. Any question from a little boy – especially a little boy from an unimportant branch of the family – would have been reacted to with derision. Even worse, it would have been treated as an act of impertinence by the august ones who organised and dominated these assemblies. For the wife of the Most August, sanctity seemed to consist entirely in bathing at regular intervals and forbidding anyone to trespass too near after she had thus purified herself. To actually touch her, accidentally or otherwise, was considered a scandalous impropriety verging on the sacrilegious. It could bring down on the offender a sudden beating and ostracism. If, embedded in all the idolatry, there were moral codes, these never penetrated to the distant benches I shared with the cousins of my own age and status where, as the pundit chanted, as the conch-horn bleated, we were pinched and cuffed into silence and submission and holy stupor.

Even now, try as hard as I might, I can discern no moral teaching, either individual or social, in our religious exercises. If, by any chance, such teaching did exist, it was not transmitted to me: somehow, I managed to miss the boat. The rites, so far as I could discern, were performed for their own sake. They were magical exorcisms, a ridding oneself of evil spirits and the summoning of benign ones. You commissioned a *puja* because you wanted yourself or someone close to you to recover from an illness, to be released from indebtedness, to pass an examination. Or, you might simply want to assure yourself of an all-pervading benevolence in the conduct of your affairs. I had relatives who did not scruple to exploit the tolerance of the Roman Catholic Church; who, without a tremor of embarrassment, boasted of the novenas they had endured. In my own home, pious as my mother was, religion was barely present. At Divali, the Hindu festival of lights, our house would be illuminated and my mother – freshly bathed, extremely stern – would prepare special vegetarian dishes which she shared with our uncomprehending neighbours. Very occasionally, we would have a *puja* in our own house. The motives for the ceremony my mother kept to herself – much as one might keep a bit of gossip to oneself. The child looked on, silent and submissive. These occasions apart, religion did not intrude.

The absence of religion in our household was matched by its absence at school. In my day – at any rate, in the institutions which I attended – we Hindu boys had no interlude set aside for religious instruction. Anglicans, Roman Catholics, Methodists, Presbyterians, Muslims . . . everyone else seemed to be provided for except us. At secondary school, every so often, one of our science teachers would appear among us abandoned ones. He talked not of sacred matters – about which, presumably, he knew nothing – but of the archaeological discoveries that had been made at Mohenjodaro and Harappa. I suppose that was his way of affirming that we too, despite all the evidence to the contrary, could lay claim to some form of existence; of pride and the self-definition necessary for it. We were not convinced. Nor, I suspect, was he. In the end, he gave up. We were surrendered to our nothingness and wandered about the playing fields pretending to relish our improbable and dubious freedom.

During adolescence I went through a phase in which I read books with a mystical bias. I waited, though without special conviction, for some blinding flash of illumination to descend upon me: the kind of thing William James had written about in *The Varieties of Religious Experience*. To enhance the possibility, I went for long walks late at night, I gazed at the stars. Of course, nothing happened. What is more, as I now realise, nothing could ever have happened. Revelations require a vocabulary. They need a context. They cannot materialise in a vacuum. Inevitably, the phase passed away. It would be easy to say that disillusionment bred scepticism. That was not the case. Scepticism implies a body of belief about which one develops doubts. What body of belief did I have to develop doubts about? My thwarted religious instincts were swallowed up in a void, were numbed into incomprehension and non-reaction. The merciless truth dawned: I had no gods of my own – was godless in the most literal sense of the term. It was a predicament beyond remedy. One consequence is that displays of piety always make me uneasy, aggravating as they do my abiding sense of being on the outside; of being a man without tribe. For gods, however universal their features, are tribal possessions. Above all else, they are totemic emblems. I am as out of place and as restless in an English country church as I am in a mosque or a temple. When I trespass into sacred precincts, claustrophobia sets in. The void, that numbed area of non-reaction, cannot be overcome.

To Tissa I said: 'I have no beliefs concerning the gods.'

'So you too have freed yourself.' He slapped my shoulders.

The passengers were beginning to return to the bus. We trailed after them. 'No,' I replied, 'I haven't freed myself from anything. I am not like you. To be a rebel – like you are – there must be something to rebel against. You had all of this . . .' We paused at the steps of the bus. I waved at the glacial dome of the temple with its gleaming spire, at the pilgrims in the courtyard with their flowers and garlands.

Tissa said, 'I do not understand.'

'Never mind. It's not all that important anyway.'

We resumed our former places, Tissa contorting himself into position beside the driver, the invalid huddling his fiery body against mine as if searching for warmth.

The countryside repeated itself. The road, winding narrowly, took us past the same bungalows with tiled roofs and little verandas, the same lanes debouching from the hinterland, the same unending stream of pedestrians and unsteady bicyclists. The driver never stopped honking his horn, though often its effect was precisely the opposite of what – presumably – was intended: the cyclists, touched with apprehension, would swerve and sway even more alarmingly. We halted frequently, losing and gaining passengers. Occasionally, the monotony was broken by our passage through some nameless, straggling township or by a vista of the grey ocean, its waves tumbling and frothing along bleak stretches of sand. Tissa read his book; the invalid, moaning and trembling, massaged his burning flesh. Our journey seemed without end.

At last, Tissa looked up at me. 'Soon we get off,' he announced. 'We find other bus.'

'Another bus!'

Tissa laughed. 'It cannot be helped.' He snapped the book shut.

'You make this trip every day?'

'Every day. What alternative is there?' He wrinkled his forehead. 'I am what you would call . . .' He paused, groping for his words. 'I am what you would call a *commuter* – is that not so?'

It would not have occurred to me that Tissa might be so described. It transformed his existence into something more comprehensible, more plausible. Tissa the Commuter – not Tissa the indigent employee of the Survey Department condemned to a life of ceaseless motion by nightmarish necessity. 'I suppose,' I said, 'You are exactly that.'

Muted amusement enlivened the eyes behind the spectacles. 'I believe there are many such in England. So at any rate I have read.' He giggled. 'Except I am not like your Mr Norris. He changes trains. I change mini-buses. It cannot be helped.' His eyes continued to glint with self-mocking amusement. 'I make this journey every day except when I am drunk.'

'What do you do when you are drunk?'

'I sleep where I fall.' Resignedly, he spread his hands. 'It has happened that I have slept on the pavement or under a bush or on a bench in a park. Does that shock you?'

'A little.'

He laughed. 'I am afraid that too cannot be helped.' His head drooped, the bony rods of his fingers dangled from his knee-caps. We had entered the outskirts of yet another nameless, straggling township. We halted. The invalid, still moaning, still trembling, was assisted down by the driver; and here we too disembarked, plunging into the dust and turmoil of noon-day. We sought the shade of the crumbling arcades, Tissa loping along with elastic strides. Stopping abruptly, he turned round to look at me. 'Arrack,' he said. 'We shall drink some arrack before going on. I would like to tell you some things. It is not to many people I can talk.' He shepherded me into a gloomily lit establishment, its floor of bare concrete, irradiated with the smells of stale food and alcohol consumption. We sat at a metal table sprinkled with grains of rice, sticky with the traces of beer, on which a colony of flies was browsing. At a nearby table a man slept, his head pillowed on his arms, his mouth agape. A boy wearing a stained apron and carrying a stained towel approached us. Yawning, he flicked at the assembled flies with his towel. They rose, circled about our heads and began settling afresh. Tissa ordered two glasses of arrack. Leaning back, he scanned my face.

'Such places I like.' There was a touch of defiance in the declaration. 'So now you see what a reprobate I am.'

I stared at the sleeping man, at the flies adventuring close to his arrack-tainted, arrack-sweetened lips.

'You are regretting . . .'

'Regretting what?' I watched a fly, bolder than the others, settle itself on the lower lip of the sleeping man. With a somnambulistic twitch and quiver of the muscles at the corner of his mouth, he succeeded in repelling the invader.

'You are regretting that you have come with me.' Tissa's voice seemed to come from a great distance.

The boy brought our drinks in glasses clouded with finger-marks.

'My wife also is regretting.' Tissa swung his torso forward, leaning his elbows on the table, meditating on the liquor visible at the bottom of the clouded glass. The noon-tide, framed by the doorway, was a glaring rectangle of heat and noise and movement. He downed his arrack in one go, dried his lips with the back of his hand, summoned the loitering boy with a click of the fingers and ordered another. 'She loves me. At night, lying with her, she tells me so and I believe her. But she is regretting she has me for a husband. I cannot blame her. It is good for you to know that before you meet her.' Tilting back his head, he swallowed the second drink as he had the first – and ordered yet another. 'How can I blame her?'

As in a dream, I saw the invalid. He floated spectrally across the luminous face of the doorway. For a moment he seemed to hang there, suspended in the glare of light and heat, before finally disappearing from view.

'Do you know how old I am?' Tissa, extending his sinuous neck, presented his face for my inspection. 'Go on. Guess.' He removed his spectacles.

Its superficial boyish raffishness evaporated under closer scrutiny. I saw the weariness in the eyes, the tortured incisions at the edges of the mouth, the coarse porousness of the skin looped over his cheekbones. His face aged as I looked at it.

'Forty . . .'

Tissa put back on his spectacles, withdrawing his head. 'I

am forty-six years old. The father of four children. For more than twenty years I have been an employee of the Survey Department. My salary after all that time is thirteen hundred rupees a month. Prospects – I have none. When the time comes, they will send me away with my pension to make room for someone else. Then there will be no more commuting.' He giggled into his privacy. 'Can you imagine what it is like to be someone like me? Can you imagine what goes on inside of here?' He pounded a fist against his head.

I was silent, dazzled by the dusty radiance lighting up the doorway. It seemed to me that I could see the after-image of the invalid hanging there.

Tissa reached forward. He touched my wrist. 'Sometimes I am so afraid.'

'Afraid of what, Tissa?'

'I do not know. I have searched for the words but I cannot find them. I cannot.' He clenched his fists. 'All I have is the fear – the pounding of the heart, the sweating in the palm, the dizziness in the head.' He took up his empty glass, revolving it in his palms. 'That is, in part, why I drink. Arrack drives away the fear. I do not drink to be happy. I drink not to be afraid.' His head drooped. 'My wife tells me that I should see a doctor.' Again he touched my wrist. 'But my fear is of the sort that no doctor can cure. That much I know.' I watched him revolve the glass. 'Shall I tell you something else?'

'Tell me.'

He revolved the glass. 'The fear is not only inside of me.' He glanced towards the doorway. 'It is *out there*. Sometimes, when I look at the ocean, I see it. It is there waiting for me in the paddy fields, in the palm groves . . .' He smiled. 'I am truly sorry. It is so hard for me to explain. I do not have the words.'

The sleeping man stirred, blinked open his arrack-bruised eyes, licked his lips and, after an instant of semi-consciousness, was reabsorbed by oblivion. Tissa gazed absently at him.

Was I able – as Tissa had asked – to imagine what went on inside of his head?

Only – I could have answered – by analogy with what went on inside of my own.

I was no stranger to the terrors he had tried to communicate. His sufferings, I divined, were not a direct result of the distempers associated with poverty, with a set of implanted ambitions strangled by straitened circumstances – bad enough though those are. Below those can lurk other, more fundamental terrors: the pervasive dread which, to a greater or lesser extent, we all share when faced with the prospect of nothingness, of formlessness, of invisibility . . . the nightmare of dissolution. The condition, for the most part heavily disguised, is often to be met with among those who have been colonised – and, by extension, among the de-tribalised. Above all, we need to exist in our own eyes; we need to have some reasonably lucid idea of what we are and who we are. (If I have made particular reference to the colonised in this regard it is only because they are close to my heart. I do not mean to suggest that our former preceptors are immune to the blight. If they had been, there would have been no temptation to dress for dinner in the middle of the jungle.) Something of the sort was happening to Tissa: he had lost his way and was no longer convinced of the reality of his existence. He was becoming invisible in his own eyes. Is there a terror greater than that? The colonised have evolved numerous strategies of evasion. I have seen the void disguised by wealth and the vulgar consumerism it encourages; I have seen it disguised by sloganeering and political extremism; I have seen it disguised by the voluptuous irrationalism of creeds like Rastafarianism. Each, rich man and Rastafarian alike, precariously perched on the edge of the abyss, frenziedly hammers together a makeshift existence, creating simulations of self-certainty. Tissa, his tribal inheritance in an advanced state of decay, was less fortunate. He had discovered no stratagems of evasion to put in its place. Adrift, dazed by his condition, he read his books and drank his arrack, tossed about on the meaningless tides of his sensations. Those sensations – unconnected, incoherent, chaotic – were all he had left. Our world is overrun with Tissas. His fate is the fate of our times. How to exist, how to become properly real – that is the question.

I listened to Tissa. He was talking of his desire to go abroad, to sell what was left of his bodily strength to the Arabs or the Nigerians. 'I wish to do so not to benefit myself but for the sake of my children. I want for them the things I do not have. I do not wish for them to be like me.'

How many times, in how many different places, had I heard those sentiments?

'What sort of work would you do?'

'Anything. I do not care. For two years I will sacrifice my pride. Many from Sri Lanka do in such countries.'

There came to mind the lament I had read in a newspaper a day or two before. 'Nigeria [ran the headline] No Paradise For Lankan Job Seekers.' A Sri Lankan migrant worker had taken the trouble to write to his Foreign Minister. 'It is the general consensus here,' he observed, 'that the days of Asians in Nigeria are numbered. In this context, I do not think it in any way advisable for Sri Lankans to venture out into Nigeria . . . the attitude of Nigerians towards expatriates, especially the coloured races, is not very encouraging . . . All of us are full of anxiety and trepidation.'

I shrank from relaying to Tissa the gist of this dismal piece of intelligence. 'Migrant workers aren't always well treated,' I said. 'You might find it a brutalising experience.'

'The brutality does not bother me, because, as I have told you, it is not for myself I wish to do it. I have heard many stories. It is the money for which I will go, the money for my children.' Tissa cracked his knuckles. 'Fact is, however, I do not think they will have me. It is only a dream.'

'What makes you say that?'

'I am too old. I should have done such a thing when I was younger.' He spread his hands. 'Of what use could I be to them? Of what use am I to anyone?' Scraping back his chair, he rose. 'We must find other mini-bus. My wife – she will worry. She will think I have fallen somewhere.' His stooped figure arched sombrely over me.

*

Tissa's house is simplicity itself: a square, shed-like structure of unplastered brick, roofed with corrugated iron and surrounded by a dusty strip of garden desultorily planted with a few scraggy fruit trees and shrubs. It is already the middle of the afternoon when we arrive. Dogs howl at us from the neighbouring yards, but do so without menace and do not stray far from the pools of shade wherein they have sought refuge. The house, though built not more than five years previously, exudes an air of neglect, of forlornness. Curtainless windows, screened by wire grids, frame the silence within. But, perhaps, my imagination exaggerates the drabness. I have been infected by Tissa's mood and by the dormancy of the afternoon through which we have walked from the main road. Tissa lifts and pushes open the wooden gate which is sagging on its hinges.

'Enter! Enter!' He urges me forward with an awkward flourish.

The room into which I am ushered is warm and airless, sparsely furnished and decorated. On the smoothly cemented floor are neither rugs nor mats. Two cane armchairs and a worn leather sofa are grouped around a low table piled with books and magazines. In one corner is a glass-doored cabinet, its shelves arrayed with a haphazard collection of table-ware. The most imposing object in the room is a plastic-topped table with chrome-plated legs. It is set out with bowls and plates and glasses, draped over with a length of mosquito netting. A couple of calendars, one Chinese, one Indian, are the sole adornments on the unpainted walls. A pair of un-shaded light bulbs dangle from flyblown cords. The asceti-cism is dismal. I see no sign of Tissa's library. That, I surmise, must be housed in one of the cubicles opening off this central space.

Tissa goes to the dining-table, lifts the mosquito netting,

makes a cursory inspection of what's hidden under it and covers it all up again. He calls out into the silence for his wife. There are stirrings in one of the cubicles. A small, pale-skinned woman, black hair tumbling down to the small of her back, dark eyes deeply recessed in their sockets, makes her entrance. Obviously, she has been dozing. When Tissa introduces us she offers a limp hand, but her eyes avoid mine.

'The food has been waiting . . .' She waves a thin arm towards the dining-table. 'It has been waiting many hours and it is now all cold.' She gazes reproachfully at Tissa – but the rebuke is tired and lacks force. She starts to twist the black cascade of her hair into a thick plait.

Tissa shuffles his feet.

'Have you been drinking arrack?' She swivels in my direction, though her eyes look past me. 'He tells me he is bringing home a guest. He tells me to cook. And then he comes when the food is cold. What am I to do?' I watch her fingers twisting and delving among the black coils.

'The food can be reheated,' Tissa says. His gaze wanders round the room, as if in search of some point of rest.

'The taste will not be the same. Your guest will form a bad opinion of me.'

Tissa's gaze continues to travel around the room, continues to fail to find for itself a congenial point of rest. Beyond the back door hibiscus and oleander glow in the sun.

Tissa slumps down on a chair. 'Where are the children?'

'They got tired of waiting for you. They have gone to see their grandmother.' She finishes the weaving of her plait; she loops it around her neck like a noose.

Tissa looks up at me. 'My mother-in-law is a good woman. I like her. Later, I shall take you to her house. It is not too far. We can walk there when it is a little cooler.'

'You like her because she spoils you.' His wife fingers the weave of her plait. 'She doesn't have to live with you.'

Tissa raises his arms as if he is about to make a protest, but then lets them fall back limply on his knees. 'That, of course, cannot be denied.' The response is flat, delivered without any hint of irony.

'I will reheat the food.' She pulls back the mosquito netting. She scowls at the bowls and plates and glasses. 'Your guest,' she says, 'might like to wash his face and hands before he eats. Not everybody can afford to be as careless as you are, Tissa.'

With effort, Tissa hauls himself to his feet. He fetches me a towel and a bar of soap still in its wrapping. 'I have told you that our facilities are not such as you might be accustomed to. You may not like . . .'

'Why should he not like?' The woman's voice echoes from the tiny kitchen. 'Do they not wash with water where he comes from?'

Tissa, impassive now, leads me out through the back door. Their water, I discover, is drawn from a well. The drought, however, has brought the well to the verge of extinction. Far down in its gloomy depths I detect a liquid gleam. Tissa lets down a bucket. The water he draws up is brown and brackish. Cautiously, I wash and soap my face, keeping my lips tightly sealed. Tissa watches me. In the kitchen, amid a rattle of crockery, his wife is singing. The thin trickle of sound meanders in the warm afternoon. 'For almost three months,' Tissa says, 'there has been no rain. Even the trees are beginning to die.' He shows me the fissured soil. Wispy clouds float high in the arid sky. A film of beige-coloured dust powders the leaves of the trees and bushes. I listen to the quavering melody emanating from the kitchen and running to seed in the drought-stricken air. 'If the rains do not come soon I do not know what we shall do.' Tissa plucks absently at the leaves of the bougainvillea.

Afterwards, we eat the reheated food – glutinous rice, curried vegetables – without appetite. Tissa uses his hands; I use the fork that has been specially provided.

'My wife too is something of a writer.' Tissa breaks the silence which has become oppressive. Inviting comment, inviting participation, he bestows on her a placatory glance.

I display suitable interest and surprise at the revelation.

But the woman, not to be persuaded into conviviality, reacts to the disclosure with embarrassment and annoyance.

'She writes many articles. Many. Why do you not show him?' Tissa licks clean his food-stained fingers.

'What is there to show him? And why should he be interested?' Listlessly, she trains her gaze on the glowing hibiscus and bougainvillea, on the well that has all but run dry. 'I am sure he cannot read Sinhalese. And, if he cannot read Sinhalese, what is the point of showing him?'

Tissa is not to be deterred. 'I will show in that case.' He runs over to the low table and gathers up an armful of the magazines stacked there. 'Her work is to be found in publications like these.' The photographs and the drawings suggest that they are women's magazines of a kind both romantic and practical in content – tales of forbidden love leavened with advice on birth-control and recipes. 'My wife also is translator,' Tissa goes on. 'She translates from the English into the Sinhalese.'

The woman scoops up the magazines. She carries them back to the low table. 'You must not listen to Tissa,' she says, flinging the words over her shoulder. 'Mainly I am a teacher. That is my job. I am a teacher of English, of geography, of history.'

'You must lead a busy life,' I hazard. Straightaway I understand that my remark is stupid and tactless.

'If I did not lead a busy life, where would I find the food to put into the mouths of my four children? Where would I find the clothes to hide their nakedness?' She keeps her back resolutely turned on me while she arranges the repossessed magazines in neat piles.

Tissa's brief spurt of effervescence is extinguished by this assault. His eyes, touched with desperation, travel round the bare walls of the room, sweep across the bare floor, seeking in vain that elusive point of rest. Head drooping, he meditates on the cracked leather of his shoes. His wife begins to clear the table, carrying the dishes to the kitchen. She resumes her joyless warbling. Outside, shadows lengthen across the drowsy afternoon.

I mention his library: to have a look at it was, after all, the ostensible purpose behind my visit.

'Ah ... my books ... my books ...' Tissa brightens. He leaps up from his chair.

He takes me into one of the cubicles. And there are his books, lining bellying planks supported on bricks, piled in heaps on the floor. The rectangular cell is furnished with a pallet, a desk over which hangs a naked bulb and a solitary wooden chair; the stumps of burned-down candles are scattered on the window-sill and protrude from the necks of empty arrack bottles encrusted with the flow of melted wax. On the wall is a framed photograph of a youthful Tissa. He is standing on a sandy beach, holding the hand of a comely young girl. Together they contemplate the ocean.

'The photograph you are looking at was taken nearly twenty-five years ago. In the month of August. On that day she and I had agreed we would become husband and wife. But that was not to happen for another three years.'

'Why was that?'

'We each wanted to complete our studies. And then what reason was there for hurry? There was so much time then.' Tissa stares at the photograph. I cannot read the expression on his face. 'My wife – she does not like to look at it. She does not like to be reminded.' Tissa paces. 'I wonder what you might have been doing on that day in August twenty-five years ago.'

I was fifteen twenty-five years ago. It being the month of August, I too may have been on a beach – a beach an ocean away. I on my beach; and Tissa, ten thousand miles away, on his, holding hands with a comely young girl. And now, this monkish cell, permeated with the musty odours of books.

'It is possible that I too was looking at the ocean.'

'And what may you have been thinking of?'

'Dreaming, maybe, of escape. I always dreamed of escape. What about you?'

'I was dreaming of being a writer.' He laughs. 'And I have gone on dreaming. I have never stopped dreaming. That has

been my problem.' He paces, waving his arms. 'However . . .
my books . . . look at my books.'

For the most part, they are ageing books. Their bindings
come apart in one's hands, the paper is brittle and yellow,
vermin have bored neatly through the pages. The books are
not arranged in any order, nor do they betray any particular
bias. Tissa seems to have acquired virtually anything that he
could lay his hands on.

'I would like to burn them.'

Startled, I turn around. His wife is standing in the
doorway.

'You may burn them on my funeral pyre,' Tissa replies.
'Not before.'

'And when will that be lighted?'

Tissa is silent; she plays with the plait looped about her
neck.

*

Later, when the sun has lost some of its ferocity, Tissa and
I set out for his mother-in-law's house. As we make our way
along the main street of the straggling village, dogs howl at us
from the sun-baked yards; children, pausing in their games,
scrutinise us; their mothers and fathers follow our progress
with restrained curiosity.

'You must forgive their inquisitiveness,' Tissa says. 'They
are trying to figure out who you are and finding themselves
unable to do so. It is not often they see strangers. Afterwards
they will enquire of my wife who you might be and why you
have come to such an out-of-the-way place.' Sometimes
Tissa's passage is acknowledged with a coy wave and a smile.
He waves and smiles back at those who greet him but does
so without especial warmth. I gather from this that his
relations with his neighbours, while cordial enough, lack any
intimacy.

Soon we come to the end of the asphalted portion of the
road. We walk now along a gravelly track. Fitful breezes
churn up clouds of white dust from its rutted surface. The

houses fall away behind us and the land opens out. Our path, winding and looping, takes us along an embankment. On either side unsown fields, sinuously veined by low ridges, stretch away into the distance – awaiting the coming of the rains. Here and there rise forested hillocks, brooding islets of green in the sere vacancy. The afternoon sun, slanting down in sheets of pale gold, lights up the crowns of the trees on the summits of the hillocks, flames on the wind-blown blades of the withered clumps of grass. Cattle and goats toil in ragged groups over the herbage. The land is lovely to look upon, elegiac in its thirsty beauty: rice lands are always beautiful, always sad.

Tissa talks again of his fondness for his mother-in-law.

'What makes you like her so much?' I watch a flock of birds swoop up from the summit of one of the hillocks, beating a black trail against the sky, going away from us.

'I like her goodness and her gentleness.'

'So you do not like her because she spoils you?'

He laughs. 'No – not because she spoils me. She accepts without anger that I have made nothing of my life. She does not hold it against me. She does not reproach me.'

The birds disappear into the brightness of the western sky. 'Isn't that a kind of spoiling?'

Tissa, bending down, plucks a blade of dried grass from the slope of the embankment. He tickles his lips with it. 'All the men in her family have made nothing of their lives. Not her father, not her husband, not her brothers, not her sons-in-law. The women have been the strong ones. It is often like that in Lanka.' Tissa lopes along beside me. Holding up the blade of grass, he lets a gust of wind sweep it away from his finger-tips. He buries his hands in his pockets. 'Is it like that in your island as well?'